Early Mourning

Early Mourning

by
Edla van Steen

Translation & Introduction by
David S. George

Latin American Literary Review Press
Pittsburgh, Pennsylvania
Series: Discoveries •1997

The Latin American Literary Review Press publishes Latin American creative writing under the series title *Discoveries*, and critical works under the series title *Explorations*.

Library of Congress Cataloging-in-Publication Data

Steen, Edla van.
   [Madrugada. English]
   Early Mourning / by Edla van Steen ; translation & introduction by
David S. George.
         p.   cm. - - (Discoveries)
   ISBN 0-935480-84-6 (alk. paper)
   I. George, David Sanderson. II. Title. III. Series.
PQ9698.29.T34M3313 1997
869.3 - -dc20

Cover design by Estúdio Noz.
Book design by Connie Mathews.

The paper used in this publication meets the minimum requirements of the American National Standard for Permanence of Paper for Printed Library Materials Z39.48-1984.∞

Latin American Literary Review Press
121 Edgewood Avenue • Pittsburgh, PA 15218
Tel. (412) 371-9023 • Fax (412) 371-9025

96-43212

Acknowledgments

This project is supported in part by grants from the National Endowment for the Arts in Washington D.C., a federal agency, and the Commonwealth of Pennsylvania Council on the Arts.

FOREWORD

Edla van Steen's 1992 *Madrugada* (*Early Mourning*) was awarded the "Coelho Neto" prize for the novel by the Academia Brasileira de Letras and, in 1993, received the Pen Club of Brazil best book award. Her 1989 play *O Último Encontro* (*The Last Encounter*) won for her the prestigious Molière and Mambembe awards for best playwright. These prizes are only the most recent in a long and distinguished career during which Edla has joined the ranks of women fiction writers and playwrights who have become major voices in Brazil.

Edla's early career included stints in broadcasting, journalism, screen writing, and stage and screen acting. For the latter, she won several awards in Brazil and abroad. Soon, however, she would relinquish her status as starlet and dedicate herself fully to writing.

She published her first book of short stories, *Cio* (*In Heat*), in 1965. Her first novel, *Memórias do Medo* (*Memories of Fear*), was published in 1974. Her second book of short stories, *Antes do Amanhecer* (*Before the Dawn*), came out in 1977. The year 1983 saw the publication of her second novel, *Corações Mordidos*, titled *Village of the Ghost Bells* in its American translation. In 1985, she published a collection of short stories entitled *Até Sempre* (*Forever*), as well as *Manto de Nuvem* (*Cloud Blanket*), a novelette for young people. She turned to playwriting with her 1989 *O Último Encontro* (*The Last Encounter*) and returned to fiction in 1992 with *Madrugada*. The year 1996 saw three new Edla van Steen books. *Cheiro do Amor* (*Fragrance of Love*), published in São Paulo by Editora Global, is a new collection of short stories. *Á Mão Armada* (*Armed Robbery*), published by Editora Caliban (São Paulo), is an adaptation for the stage of her novel *Madrugada*. *Por Acaso* (*By Chance*), her second novelette for young people, was published by Editora Global (São Paulo).

Many other Edla van Steen stories have appeared in Brazilian collections and magazines. Her fiction has been translated into several languages, including Italian, German, Polish, Spanish, and English. American translations include an anthology of her stories published under the title *A Bag of Stories* (David S. George trans., Latin American Literary Review Press, 1991), as well as her novel *Village of the Ghost Bells* (David S. George trans., U. of Texas Press, 1991). Other Edla van Steen short stories have been published in such venues as *Sudden Fiction International* (W.W. Norton, 1989), *One Hundred Years After Tomorrow* (Darlene Sadlier ed, Indiana U Press, 1991), *The Literary Review*, and *The Latin American Literary Review*. Finally, her fiction and drama have been examined in hundreds of reviews, scholarly articles, dissertations, and books.

Edla has three children. The eldest, Ricardo, as well as her youngest daughter, Léa, are film directors. Her oldest daughter, Anna, also works in the cinema. Her husband, Sábato Magaldi, is Brazil's foremost theater critic. The author has one grandchild. Her home in São Paulo sits high on a hill overlooking the city, and like the traffic helicopter in *Early Mourning* it provides a panoramic view of the city; it also affords a glimpse into Edla van Steen's fiction. The astonishing mélange of paintings covering the walls and sculptures dispersed throughout the house and the yard reflect her profound love and knowledge of the visual arts. One of the pleasures of reading her work is its visual quality. *Early Mourning* is no exception. The narrative is a wry danse macabre that winds its way through the streets of São Paulo to a funeral parlor where all segments of society come together: wealthy and poor, city slickers and rural bumpkins, cops and robbers, Italians and Japanese, circus clowns and striptease artists. *Early Mourning* filters the universal themes of death and renewal through the lens of Brazil's urgent social problems. In a single night, from sundown to early morning, the reader soars on the polar wings of laughter and pathos over a vast urban landscape drenched in the deep red of a dying sun and bids farewell to a memorable gallery of characters on the dew–brushed ground of Memorial cemetery.

Edla has written several screenplays. It should come as no surprise, then, that *Madrugada* began life as a film script. Her children, as the reader will imagine, provided input. Its cinematic sweep over São Paulo, its jump–cutting, its dazzling array of lighting effects, its cops–and–robbers motif linger in the book's atmosphere. But its novelistic features, its narrative twists and multiple points of view, drew Edla back to fiction. And adapting it to the stage was not an unnatural turn in the work's contorted genesis.

It has been for me a great satisfaction to be involved in the *Madrugada* project, as its translator and co–adaptor to the stage. My association with Edla is long–standing and multifaceted. I have published translations of her work, which are listed above. I have written and spoken about her fiction and drama in scholarly journals and conferences. As a college teacher, I have taught her works in my courses. Edla has helped me gain access to writers and to the publishing market in Brazil. We have, in short, collaborated on a great variety of projects, large and small. Most important, we have been friends since 1969, when I was a wide–eyed Fulbrighter in Brazil and she was beginning her literary career. For a friendship to evolve into a professional partnership, while remaining true to its origins, is surely one of life's blessings. And as long as she has books to write, I have translations to make. And miles to go before we sleep. There will be no early mourning for us.

David S. George
Evanston, June 1996

This translation is dedicated to
Bia Zonis and Alex George.

1

On Thursday, the thirteenth day of September, at four o'clock in the afternoon, the first car leaves the garage. The old lady on the corner crosses herself, thinks, "there but for the grace of God go I," walks across the street, and notices the van parking down the street and the brazen hussy's proposition. Is nothing sacred anymore, not even a hearse?

He's come to pick up the body on one of those quiet streets lined on both sides with trees and turn-of-the-century mansions. The few apartment complexes, of recent construction and built on the back of the lots, have underground garages disguised with a covering of plants. No, the driver has no problem finding a parking space in front of the luxurious home where Giuseppe Appia's relatives have come to view his body. This is an emotional time; they're all grieving and lining up to approach the coffin. Someone can be heard explaining:

"The police have just released the body, twelve hours after... Senseless... The poor family."

The widow's face is so far inscrutable, as if the deceased had no relation to her. "She's in shock," a neighbor lady thinks, before mentioning that the widow and her husband had four children. Luigi, the eldest, the one over there in the corner of the room with his arms around two young children, works with his father at the Gothic Construction Company. Joel, the second son, opted for dentistry and never married. Odd, shy, he's out on the porch chain smoking. Marina and that blond fellow are newlyweds. They look so sad, whoever would have expected... The youngest daughter, Francesca, that's a portrait of her over there by the sofa, was always very attached to her father but she won't be at the wake. There's no time, she's studying acupuncture in Japan, and what would be the point? That other photograph shows three generations of Appias on their grandfather's ninetieth birthday. It was taken in the same room where the grandson's body is on view. No one could ever have imagined that someday Bepi would kill himself with a bullet to his chest. No one.

The phone rings and the sound seems too real for this atmosphere of bewilderment.

"Yessir. No, the wake will be at cemetery. He'll be going soon, the hearse is waiting outside."

Outside the house, the driver smiles in deep satisfaction. A passerby would even say that... Can you believe your eyes? My god, all hell's going to break loose if anyone goes up to talk to him. Hey, driver. Listen here. How could you think of doing such a thing on this street, in broad daylight, in that kind of vehicle? The coffin'll be here any minute. Please. Look back there. That's right. You see? He straightens up and tries to look dignified as he grasps the steering wheel and struggles to keep the uncooperative woman's head out of sight.

The coffin is raised with difficulty, dragged into the back of the hearse, and the rear door slams shut. The driver waits only a few seconds before he speeds off to the dismay of the family members, who race to keep up with the funeral procession.

In the hearse, the woman finally sits up and straightens her hair.

"Jeez, man. I almost suffocated." She wipes her mouth, smeared with lipstick. And they both break into laughter.

Imagine the city with this late-afternoon red color, seen from way up in the buildings on Avenida Paulista, or from the helicopter flying over it. Who could feel unmoved at a time like this? Every day Giuseppe Appia, that is, Bepi, took the same route to work. He usually arrived before his employees because he liked to read the newspaper, undisturbed, in his office. Wasn't a single person who didn't find him interesting, in spite of his sixty years. São Paulo was his favorite city. He'd never live anywhere else. Just like his grandfather, who passed through in 1900 on a trip from Italy and never went back. They say he fell in love with a member of São Paulo's upper crust, a woman in her forties, older than he, married. He wasn't the first one to fall for her, but he wished to be the last. How could a husband leave his wife alone in the city and choose to live far from her, on a plantation? A fine specimen like her? Sure, she had to look after their children's education, and he had to look after the family's wealth. What's more, there was no evidence she ever had a lover. None. Oh, people can be so vindictive—her fidelity was questioned. The Italian bent to the task: he began courting her openly, at a party. She was absolutely irresistible for a man from a small town in Lucania, invited by a cousin who had become a prosperous textile manufacturer overnight. What a bounteous country Brazil was in those days. What women! The city's muse ignored his courtship and actually threw her oldest daughter into his arms, not quite so fetching, as they said in those days, but attractive nonetheless. He married the daughter, Maria Alcinda de Queiroz Bueno e Silva, and founded the Brazilian branch of the Appias with her. A few friends, filled with admiration and jealousy, swore that to his dying day he screwed both of them, mother and daughter. An exemplary Italian macho. Hanging on some wall of the house there must be a photograph of him, arms linked with the two of them. Bepi bore a striking physical resemblance to his grandfather, who also appreciated the late afternoon view from the office window...

The hearse stops at a corner, next to a newsstand. The woman, squeezed into a velvet miniskirt, gets out slowly. One hand holds her purse and coat and the other, wrapped around the money the driver has given her, waves good-bye.

"See you tomorrow. You know where to find me."

Construction on Avenida Paulista holds up the slow-moving traffic even more. He tries to shut out those gaunt, lined faces queued up at the busstops. Faces stamped with sadness and worry. Faces of a people who have run out of luck. The driver turns on the radio full volume: the sound of jazz graces the world with its vibrant Brazilian saxophone.

The stoplight suddenly changes. The van brakes violently in the middle of the intersection and crashes into a white Mercedes.

"It's nothing serious." The driver, short and potbellied, dressed in an ill-fitting navy blue suit, cap askew on his head, tries to act polite and dignified. "The funeral home will pay for any damages, sir. The light changed so fast. Excuse me, but I have to deliver the body."

The fellow is plainly nervous.

"Where's the funeral procession? I don't see anyone following you. We've got to report this to the police. This is all I needed. I've never seen a funeral procession without anyone in it..."

"I lost it in traffic. It's someone named..." He checks his pockets for the name, finds a piece of paper, tries unsuccessfully to read it. "I always forget the dead guy's name."

The other man slaps himself on the forehead.

"Oh, no. Bepi? I know him! He died, just like that? For Pete's sake, we had lunch together less than a week ago. I thought he seemed kind of down, but for him to die..."

The traffic cop orders them to stop arguing and move on. Can't they see they're blocking traffic?

Thanks to the accident, the Appia family procession catches up with the body and is able to accompany it to the cemetery. Every cloud has a silver lining.

The open casket has been placed on a silver pedestal. Beside it, a tall crucifix and candelabra. Four tapers have been lighted. The funeral home has done everything right—the company secretary reflects. What if something had gone wrong?

There are six parlors reserved for wakes, all more or less alike. The first one to the right off the hallway is reserved for Giuseppe

Appia. The one the left is occupied: a man, not identified by a name-plate or in the guestbook. The coffin isn't made of hardwood like the businessman's, there's no crucifix, decorations, or silver candelabra, the secretary notices, before heading for the coffee shop at the end of the hallway. Let the Appia family hang around listening to condolences from their friends. She'll have some coffee and smoke a cigarette. After all, she's had no rest since the boss's desperate act. All that moaning and groaning is getting on her nerves. Mio Bepi, che cosa ha fatto. My Bepi, what have you done?

The relatives are arriving: cousins, uncles and aunts, in-laws.

"Wakes begin and end the same way," sighs Elias, the guard on duty.

Japa, washing coffee cups, agrees with a nod of his head. He is a short fellow, stocky like someone who spends the day body building; his face, expressionless. It would be hard to guess his age. He hasn't had any sleep because he's been working at the counter for two shifts—he needs the money.

"Never fails."

2

On that same Thursday the thirteenth, at four thirty in the afternoon, the circus isn't full, but it's not a bad house. Like all Thursday matinees. The midgets finish their balancing act and frolic to enthusiastic applause. It's time for the clown act.

Backstage, the cyclist who rides the globe of death is arguing with Irene, the trapeze artist, so slender in her green satin tights.

"You're too drunk to go on, Alfredo. How about a cup of coffee?"

Alfredo staggers to his motorcycle but manages to climb on. Irene anxiously signals to Tiny, the midget, who has stopped to observe the scene.

"Please, call Menendez."

The midget runs out, crawls under the canvas, and proceeds to the ticket booth where the boss is adding up the receipts. On his way there he motions to Paquita, who oversees the circus from a window.

"Irene needs you, Menendez. Alfredo's screwed up again. And he wants to do his act."

Menendez looks at the circus ring: the clowns are just beginning. The audience is enjoying the twin brothers. Especially the mirror act, on opposite sides of an empty frame, one of them handsome and the other ugly. Their gestures are so perfectly symmetrical!

"Those boys are good. I grew up in the circus, I know what I'm talking about. They're going to go far." He puts the receipts away in the drawer and slips the money into his pocket. "Let the magician know he'll have to go on and tell the twins to stretch things out."

Tiny stays put, expecting him to take action.

"I'm on my way. I've got to close the ticket booth and take the dough to Paquita. I'll be there in five minutes."

The midget's only fifty something, but he looks much older with that face like an underfed monkey. A shrewd look on his face, he runs off.

When the magician hears the door slam he stops applying his white make-up and asks who is it without looking away from the mirror.

"Menendez asked you to hurry up and go on before the globe, 'cause Alfredo's smashed."

"That guy's hopeless. This's been happening every week for who knows how long."

The midget doesn't argue and tries on a white glove.

"My glove!" The magician shouts. "Are you nuts?"

Tiny smiles, squints his near-sighted eyes, and apologizes.

"Look at the sunset. The color's something."

Menendez also notices when he closes the ticket booth. Red skies make him melancholy. Any day now some important circus will discover those twins and that'll be the end of the Menendez success, three generations, from father to son. Diego learned how to do pantomime, ride horseback, and sit in Nero's lap—a huge bear that pedaled a bicycle while feeding him with a bottle—even before the boy knew how to speak. He fondly remembers Karl, the tamer-mime-singer, who was the star in his father's time. A stingy German who wouldn't let himself spend a penny unless it was absolutely necessary. One day he gave Nero to his assistant and said goodbye.

"I must return to my Germany. Zat is vere I vant to die."

All Diego's efforts were to no avail, though he spent hours on

Nero's lap. The bear just missed Karl too much. Believe it or not, Diego saw Nero cry several times. He'd lift up that heavy paw and wipe his face like an adult human. At those times Diego would sit on his lap and give him a kiss, a loud smack—the sound delighted Nero. But nothing worked: he died of longing for the tamer a few months later. The circus lost a good part of its audience, but won it back when the twins joined up.

When he turned eighteen Diego took over to help his mother, burdened with the problems caused by his father Josef Menendez's binges. That was a fatal flaw for a manager. How could he command respect?

Paquita, a first-class fire-eater, tried to be everywhere at once. Descended from Gypsies, she smooth-talked the artists when they asked for a raise. Through daily pilfering from the box-office, she paid lower rent for the lots where the circus was set up.

Every day Diego watched his mother show the landlords the number of tickets sold and carry on about her rotten luck.

"I swear. On my son's honor. We lead a hard life. We keep going because we're artists. The circus ring is our home. The only thing we could change is moving to another circus. You understand?"

Paquita's husband figured out the hiding place for her savings—a pillow—and while his wife performed her act he would go to the trailer and steal enough for some rum. Those were occasions when Diego had a great time. He deeply admired his father, a cheerful man who sang beautiful Spanish songs. His mother wouldn't let him go out alone.

"So he doesn't do anything stupid. A man worth his salt doesn't teach his son to be a good-for-nothing."

And off the two of them would go to the cathouse. Afterwards they'd go shopping and fill up the old panel truck at the marketplace. And on the way back, down the road they'd sing. Diego also cheats his mother now and then by stealing from the box-office. He hides the money in a shoe. Like father like son.

She hasn't been out of the trailer in four years: she had a tumor removed from her stomach and her love for fire-eating went with it. But she enjoys adding up the receipts, and so the first thing Diego does is hand over the bills and coins to her.

"A gorgeous sunset," he exclaims. The late afternoon sun casts an orange glow on the tent; it looks new. Diego sighs: he ought to get married. There are times—like this red sunset—when he longs for a wife and kids. Why is that?

"What's wrong? Small crowd?"

"Alfredo drank too much but he insists on doing his act."

His mother is watching television. A western. Everybody praises her trailer, lined with printed cloth. And Diego likes the family portrait—she, his father, and he in the middle, in his sailor suit. He remembers Josef Menendez, drunk, being carried home. Paquita eating fire in the circus ring. Fat, bleached blond, an open and healthy face, acknowledging the applause and then running off to take care of her husband. Why did circus people drink? Such a cruel fate. Her son would not inherit his father's vice. No, he would not.

"The motorcycle act?" She asks.

"Yup. He found out Irene's having an affair with one of the clowns, Sandro. We'll talk about it later."

"You took care of your father. You're an expert when it comes to drunks."

Paquita will soon turn sixty; he's almost forty. They share birthdays. Diego slams the trailer door and for a moment recalls the terrible scene: his father, in the middle of the street, run over. As if it had just happened.

The clown act is drawing to a close. The audience applauds. Drum rolls announce the globe of death. The cyclist suddenly revs the motor.

"Make up your mind. Him or me?" He looks groggily at the trapeze artist.

Irene is confused, speechless. But when she hears him drive away she screams:

"For god's sake, no!"

Too late. He drives into the ring, circles it once, and enters the globe. The drum rolls get louder. Some members of the audience watch with their mouths open as the metallic ball goes up and down. Irene runs over to Sandro. Having just completed his act, he's totally in the dark.

"It's Alfredo... He's..."

The grating sound of the motorcycle crashing and the silence of the drums announce the tragedy. Women and children scream. Pandemonium at the circus.

Irene cries in Sandro's arms.

"How can we ever be happy after this?"

"There, there, darling. There, there."

A doctor in the house rushes to the aid of the accident victim. He shakes his head. Alfredo is dead.

The proper measures must be taken—Diego signals to the midget and they silently leave together in the old panel truck. They don't talk as they drive along; each keeps his feelings to himself. Tiny is in agony.

He feels a great loss for what he never had, if that makes sense to anyone. His mother died in childbirth. She never saw the son who had to be bottle fed by his aunt, an old maid. Is it possible she offered him her dried-up breast to experience the sensation of having a child? It could be, but he has no recollection. The name on his birth certificate was Xandó Vieira, but it made no difference. He always has been and will be called Tiny. He took the nickname in the right spirit and made it his stage name: Tiny Vieira. He has two older brothers of normal height who live in a small town. He never looks them up so as not to put them in an uncomfortable position. One is a congressional candidate and it wouldn't help if he showed up. Meanwhile, this is his family—the circus. Until he gets married and has his own family. Should that ever come to pass.

The casket company offers several options: the coffins, all in a row, shown by an insolent salesman.

"This one here's for people who can afford it." He points to a hardwood casket. "It costs more'n all three of us put together make in a whole year. The one you want's back there."

And he is in fact right. Prices in back are significantly lower. Tiny climbs up on a chair, examines the model on display, and points to a lilac-colored coffin. He suddenly finds himself thinking that there aren't any caskets his size here. Maybe in the kids' section.

Diego signals for the midget to come over.

"How tall is Alfredo?"

"Twice my height. We measured each other once. I'm sure of it."

"Make it another two inches. Dead people stretch," the circus owner adds.

"And all this time I thought they shrunk," Tiny replies ironically.

While they wait for the coffin to be loaded into the panel truck, Diego leans against the door with his head hanging down.

"We can't even afford to die anymore. Did you see what that cheap pine cost?"

The midget nods.

"Anyone works for me deserves a proper burial. I am right or what? Not to mention he's an artist. I'm gonna bury him next to my father."

"Take it easy, Menendez. The coffin's fine."

"We'll have the wake at the cemetery. Ok. That's that."

Back at the circus, the body is laid out on a platform for viewing. No one has changed clothes. The loin tamer takes off his cape and covers Irene, whose head is on Sandro's shoulder. The red ball is still stuck on his nose. The elephant is sad. So is the lion. Nothing looks more desolate than an empty circus. The patches look huge—Tiny notes. Who'd have the nerve to go up to the casket? It looks so plain and forlorn.

One of the trapeze artists summons the magician, who's having a brandy.

"Life's worthless, honey." He glances over at the dead man, who looks so defenseless. He lets go of the monkey clinging to his neck—his beloved Gina—and makes a grand gesture. He pulls flowers from his pockets, sleeves, and top hat and goes about decorating the coffin with them. The circus folk are overjoyed. That's precisely what was missing—Gina claps and turns somersaults. The flowers!

Diego Menendez brings the mother slowly in. She's so fragile, considering her two hundred and some pounds. She's put on makeup, as if she were about to perform. Her hair swept back and fastened with a black ribbon. What a beautiful woman she must have been.

"Congratulations"—she greets the magician. "Let's go, folks. The truck is ready."

3

More and more people arrive at Bepi Appia's wake. Now it's the people from the office offering their condolences to the family. Another body lies alone in an empty parlor, the guestbook unsigned. Elias, the guard on duty, inspects the coffin. Wonder who it is. Looks like a foreigner. Don't remember ever seeing a body left alone like that. Maybe folks'll be showing up soon. The law says you can't be buried till a relative gives authorization. Anyway, somebody must've got the body ready and rented the parlor—he decides to go out to the sidewalk. Sunsets like this make him restless. He looks up.

Brenda smiles and waves to him from the window. She goes to the mirror to put on her makeup. Tight black slacks and white blouse. Black eyeliner and green eyeshadow highlight her eyes and a light shade of lipstick brightens her lips. Finally, she combs her hair and puts on a wig—short, straight, dark-brown hair. Or should she wear the blond wig? She tries it on. No, she prefers the other one.

"Well, doll, today's the day." She winks at herself, feigning indifference, but she just felt a pang in her stomach. Every time she has to face a new situation she gets an upset stomach. A burning sensation. She opens the refrigerator, grabs a bottle of milk, and takes a swig. That usually helps a little. How about calling someone? There's a whole bunch of people she owes a phonecall. It seems like forever since she's talked to her friends. She doesn't have the time, or the desire—she picks up the phone. Her only wish is to take off for the United States. But she doesn't want to lose her apartment; it's small and cozy, with those posters of pop star Roberto Carlos and the transvestite Roberta Close—she tells herself, before dialing a number.

"Hello, is it you?... Are you busy?... I cleaned house yesterday. I love household stuff... (She looks around, satisfied) I'm a cancer... Sure, you have keep things orderly... You do what you can... No, thank goodness I've had everything I've needed... Knock on wood... Not even when my father... I'm not going get off on that subject... Mamma? Of course, she was a big help with decorating and dishes. She's not like those parents who don't accept their children for what they are... If she won the lottery... It's a drag when you don't have enough money... I've got a plan. If it works, I'm gonna say goodbye to this horseshit lifestyle. A good plan. I mean, if the club closes, you know, everybody's broke... (She begins pacing around the room) If it happens, that's it for any chance of some bigshot agent or tv producer's seeing my show. Not too many people do what I do, right?.. Thanks, honey, I know you appreciate me... I don't think so. Elvis Presley and João Gilberto are my best impersonations, but the boss prefers my Frank Sinatra. Just like you... (She wets a finger with tongue and rubs her eyebrows) I do the act for him, because the customers don't care for it... What're you gonna do? Can't please everyone... If I were in the United States. Now there's a country... (She's just got to stop biting her nails. She inspects them. Ugh) I can't stop thinking about going... I've got the name of an agent now... I know it's full of Brazilians. All the more reason... Ok, I'll wait for you on Sunday. It's the old man's birthday. Are you going to the penitentiary with me?... Thanks. See you."

Brenda hangs up the phone, considers making another call, and notices the sun. Oh, she hates being alone for a sunset like this... She feels so strange... The walls are rosy pink. Cool—she looks down.

Elias is waiting, watching... She gestures for him to come up.

But he has to wait a few more minutes for his relief. This month he's on the day shift. Better than the night shift. He's the opposite of Brenda. If she could she'd sleep all day and wouldn't wake up till six in the evening. A night owl. But he likes daylight, sun, heat. When he thinks about snow in the United States he shivers! No way he'd go. Not a chance. He's got an ace in the hole. If Brenda's set to go and if nothing else works, he'll ask her to marry him. He's ok with night-club shows. After all, he can't stop her from working. But if she ends up in some other country... What would he do there? He's not about to give up his police work for a woman. He just can't. Even if she were the most famous actress in the world. Brenda deserves a lot of credit, even as a keener, but... The dead man for sure's got someone to cry over his death. At least one: her.

His relief arrives, almost at a run.

"Sorry I'm late. There's some construction on Paulista tying up traffic."

"See you tomorrow. Isn't that sunset something?"

"Sure is."

Elias crosses the road, turns the corner, and goes into Brenda's building.

4

It's what Nando was hoping would happen; the watch is chang-
ing.

One is leaving, the other's having a beer, and he's calmly entering Memorial Cemetery. He has some coffee and a piece of cake for
Dito. So sick, poor fella.

The light casts a red glow on the imposing shrines; Nando pauses
before the sculpture of a sleeping woman. It's his favorite. He never
fails to stop and admire the reclining woman, wearing a sort of tunic,
her arms flung wide as if she were about to make love. Her wavy hair
falls over her small breasts. Her eyes and mouth: enraptured. Nando
feels the urge to lie on top of her—he runs his hand tenderly down
her arm. At that hour, with that light, you'd think she's alive. He then
stops in front of the chair. Some gentle soul thought of having an
empty chair sculpted, in recognition of the loved one not there. It
must have been a blue velvet chair, he thinks, like the one in the
corner shopwindow.

Nando picks a lily from one of the graves and observes his long

Edla van Steen

thin shadow. How old is he? Thirty? Forty? He pauses before a large
family crypt, a chapel, one of those with halls that lead to two or
three wings containing the vaults. The door is ajar. Written above it:
Alvar...Family—the rest of the name has worn away over time.

Before entering, Nando looks up again at the sky: gorgeous!

"I brought you a flower." He bends down and hands it to Dito,
who is lying on a pile of cardboard boxes. "How you feel? Any better?"

Dito squeezes his eyes shut in appreciation. He is visibly fever-
ish as he shivers with cold despite the blankets.

Nando places a pan of water on the burner.

"I'm going to make some coffee for us. Where're the matches?"
He looks for them among the aluminum mugs and plates.

"In your pocket," Dito whispers.

Nando laughs.

"We never think of the obvious place." He sits on the real mat-
tress, which belongs to him. "Don't you want to lie on my bed?"

"No. I know you don't like it."

"But you're sick."

The effort to speak brings on one of Dito's coughing spells.
Nando pretends he doesn't notice and waits for the coughing to stop.
He opens a bottle of rum, gives his friend a drink, and sits back down.
He's gotten worse. It started with a simple cold and now he's been
burning up with fever for several days. Or could it be weeks? Nando
doesn't know anymore. Their hangout is the entrance to the cemetery. Dito was the first to arrive. He claimed it was his territory, but
he didn't mind sharing it with someone else. People feel safer when
there's someone to take care of their cars, especially at night when
they give fat tips. And he could use some company.

"I wish my mother could come from up north. There's a little
place just like ours over on the next row she could stay in."

Nando turns happily to his friend. They rarely speak. Maybe he
really is getting better.

"Do you remember her?"

"Who?"

"Your mother."

Dito breathes deeply. He seems tired.

36

"A little. I remember her smell the best. Rose water."

"I never saw my mother or my father," Nando says. He takes a swig of rum. "I was raised in an orphanage, but the government shut it down and I've been living in the streets ever since."

He stands up, puts instant coffee in the mugs, and to pour the boiling water he grabs a rag hanging on a clothesline stretched between two high vaults.

"It think you're a swell person," Dito says with difficulty, while his friend helps him raise his head slightly to drink the coffee.

"I wouldn't know what a real house is like. Once this lady wanted to adopt me, but it didn't work out. I guess she got scared off. I wasn't too hot in the bathing department."

Dito laughs and starts coughing again.

"I'm not going make it through the night."

"Knock it off, Dito. There's a real important wake today. At least we can earn a little change early tomorrow morning."

The invalid stares dejectedly at his friend.

"I had a dog and a burro up north in Pernambuco. Sometimes I dream I'm riding it or I'm swimming in the river. And I wake up feeling happy."

Dito coughs uncontrollably. Nando covers him affectionately.

"Hush. Don't talk any more. Get some rest."

5

The video rental shop is located in their home, a two-story house in the Itaim district. The general situation had gone from bad to worse and the multinational corporation laid off Sérgio and Maria Sampaio. All they had to do was move up to the second floor and use the equity from their retirement fund to set up their small business downstairs. It's a temporary solution. There aren't any video stores in the neighborhood, and this way they can care for their ten-year-old daughter. Frail and wan, she sits in the corner watching "Fantasia". It's her favorite movie, thinks her mother, as she checks the quality of an order in the next room. Ten years ago today, September thirteenth, at this exact time, she was entering a church. The sunset wasn't as spectacular—she looks out—but the rain seemed to have stopped just so she wouldn't get mud on her wedding gown. A sumptuous wedding. When she said "I do," white rose petals began falling from the ceiling while the chorus sang the theme song from "Love Story." The honeymoon in Miami was a gift from the company. What Brazilian firm would do a thing like that? They liked working for the Americans. The employees were always rewarded for their efforts. No, they never imagined that one day they'd be sent packing, just like that, casualties of cost control. To be honest, she and her husband are tired of working until late at night, without overtime, because their own employees fail to show up or it's the Christmas season and the sale of electronic equipment is up. No, they never imagined anything so absurd. Particularly during an economic crisis, a few months after they discovered Beatriz had leukemia. When it rains it pours—her mother used to say. Turns out she was right.

A customer comes into the store, returns a tape, and requests another, which Sérgio looks for on the shelf.

"Do you know if "Fantasia" is out?"

"No," Maria answers. "Ask Bia."

Sérgio goes over to his daughter, who seems to be sleeping, and ejects the tape.

"Please, Dad. Leave it in."

"You've seen "Fantasia" ten times. And your eyes were shut."

"I can picture it all in my mind."

"I know, honey. But there's a customer asking for it... Be nice. I'll pick out another movie for you."

"But I'm in the middle."

"You can watch the rest of it tomorrow."

He removes "The Love Bug" from the shelf, hands it to his daughter, and kisses her on the forehead.

"I'm sorry. I love you, you know."

She gives her father a that's-not-fair look. His daughter's displeasure almost makes him change his mind. But this is a video rental store and the customers come first.

A half hour later, the mother, who is checking several video tapes at once, asks her husband if he's given Bia her medicine.

"I can't stop working now. The pills are over the kitchen sink."

He checks a bill of sale from the importer, but he'll go soon, his wife shouldn't worry.

Finally, Maria stands up, her hands on her back.

"I'm bushed... I need a hot bath... That's enough for today." She goes over to her daughter's wheelchair. "Isn't that movie funny, Bia?"

No answer.

"Hey, honey, are you sleeping?"

She picks up her limp hand and is terrified. There is no pulse.

"Sérgio! Please. Call the doctor. Quick. Bia... Bia..."

There are times you understand what has happened but you can't accept it. Beatriz has had leukemia since the age of seven. They've done everything they could—the girl attended school until two months ago—in the hope her system would respond, or that fate would hold a pleasant surprise for the Sampaio family. Why not? Medical history is full of unexplained cases of recovery. Beatriz, unfortunately, will not be so lucky.

The white coffin is late on its way to the wake at Memorial Cemetery.

"I think a child died in that house," Mara, the traffic news reporter, tells the helicopter pilot.

São Paulo is magnificent in the fading light. The sky has turned purple. It's a rare spectacle for the reporter and the pilot.

"What a day," she remarks. "For summer. Makes you want to do who knows what. Follow the Beltway to the Morumbi bridge. Let's see what's cookin'. What time is it?"

"We won't be on the air for another fifteen minutes."

"Then turn up the radio. I'm nuts about Paulo Moura."

The pilot glances longingly at his partner. For a good while now he's wanted to get close to that short, high-strung woman, with the constantly wide-open dark eyes. But he doesn't dare. What if she were annoyed? He admires her thick, straight Indian hair.

"You married?"

The sudden interest takes her by surprise.

"I was. How about you?"

"No. Thank my lucky stars. I lived with a woman from down south for four years. One day I showed up unannounced."

"She was with another man, right?"

"Wrong. It was a woman."

She laughs. She takes notes on the traffic. The helicopter follows its designated route. The swimming pools are filled. Discreetly, she looks at the pilot as if she were seeing him for the first time. About forty, and if he didn't have this thing about not shaving he'd be attractive, in spite of his being overweight. He's not the man of her dreams, but he'll do. He reminds her a bit of her ex-husband: the same vulnerable look, the dirty fingernails, the hair that needs trimming. And he smokes too much... She can't stand smoker's breath. But she can't deny that she's feeling very attracted to him. Aroused by the sunset. That light is so...so... peculiar. That's it.

"What about you? Been divorced for long?"

"Not divorced yet. Not till next month. I've been separated for three years."

"Incompatibility?"

"Not at all. We got along like brother and sister. We got married too fast. We didn't give the relationship a chance to develop. We were both workaholics. And that was that as far as the marriage went."

The radio announcer informs them he's about to call the helicopter. She'll be on the air in fifteen seconds.

"Only a few bottlenecks in São Paulo today. A stoplight is out at the intersection of Cidade Jardim and Faria Lima. There are traffic delays on Paulista and on Rebouças heading south, near Clínicas Hospital, which you can avoid by taking Cardeal Arcoverde. It's a pleasant afternoon, with clean air and clear skies. This is Mara Domingues for Pinheiros Radio."

"You up for a beer?" The pilot asks, wearing a mischievous expression.

She accepts. This sure is an unusual day for the polluted, dingy city.

6

It's getting dark out. With a pass of a magic wand, presto, a thousand lights have been turned on. Brenda—on the way to the bar to meet someone—feels this isn't the first time she's experienced the sensation that the city is connected to a single outlet and everything lights up at once. A childish sensation. She feels small, almost like a baby in her mother's arms. She never understood why her mother smelled like garlic, even when she wasn't cooking. She was a tall woman with huge breasts like an Italian actress. Everything about her was large: her mouth, nose, eyes. When they went to mass together on Sundays Brenda observed her mother's rearend swinging from side to side and felt ashamed of all that loose flesh. She recognized the men's lust as they turned their heads to stare at her ample behind waddle along. Brenda would starve to death before she'd ever let her body get like that. Whenever she feels tempted to eat she summons up the image of her mother. Let them complain that she's too thin, that she has a man's voice and body: she doesn't care. Elias likes her. Too bad her affair with him is getting so mixed up. She

47

thinks she could fall in love but she doesn't want to. She needs to-tal—including emotional—independence to carry out her plans. She can't afford romantic complications at a time like this, when she's close to realizing her dream. She must concentrate on her hate for the world, for men. Has she forgotten everything?

No, that's not something you forget. Ten years old. She was standing in the doorway of the blue house in Água Branca. Geraniums in the windows. That day, the neighbor woman's daughter came over to spend the afternoon with her. A hot day. They had bought some ice cream and they stood in the doorway talking about school, their classmates, and the neighborhood. The company car from her father's office pulled up.

A man in suit and tie, carrying a briefcase, approached them.

"Is this Ademar Santos's house?"

"Yes. But he's at work," Brenda answered politely.

The man gave her a smug grin.

"Precisely. He hasn't shown up and I've been sent here to inquire. Is your mother home?"

"No. She's gone out."

The man looked up and down the street, saw no one was watching from a nearby window, went back to the car, spoke to his companion, and returned.

"May I come in and wait? I need to speak with him urgently and it's a long drive over here. You're Brenda, aren't you?"

She was reluctant to let a stranger in, but if he knew her name he must be an acquaintance of her father. She opened the door and noticed him signal to the other man in the car. Brenda and her friend (she can't recall her name today; suddenly forgetting someone's name happens to her sometimes) sat primly on the living room couch and the man chose a chair near the table.

"Would you like anything, sir?"

"A glass of water."

Brenda went to the kitchen. The visitor pretended to look nonchalantly around the house. She selected a saucer to put under the glass; she'd been properly taught, and the man would praise her manners when he saw her father. She noticed the man tremble as he took the glass.

"You think I might ask your friend to take a glass out to the man in the car?"

The other girl got up and went out compliantly without looking back. Brenda suddenly felt afraid. The man, breathing heavily, moved from the chair to the sofa.

Brenda cringed in the other corner.

"If you're a nice girl, nothing will happen to your father. I won't let them send him away. I'll arrange it all with the company. What about it, hm?" A slimy hand grabbed her around the waist.

No, stop. That's all she manages to remember. She can't and won't think about that monster who fell on top of her. Because the truth is she can't admit even to herself without some discomfort that she came when she was raped. At ten years of age. She screamed with pleasure. Which horrified the man. That naked girl, who didn't even have breasts yet, languid with pleasure, wasn't a child any-more—he dressed hurriedly and fled.

When her father found out about it he didn't think twice. He bought a pistol and tried to kill the man, shooting him at close range. But the fellow was rescued in time and he survived. Her father waited for him to get out of the hospital and he shot him again. The newspapers at the time described the incident as the settlement of a gambling dispute. Brenda (named after a singer her mother was a fan of) grew up with the secret on the other side of the city to avoid wagging tongues. Her father is still in prison. He got a jury that was fed up with the crime wave in São Paulo and they made him a scapegoat.

Brenda goes into the bar, where Oswaldo and Teleco are drinking beer.

"Hi, how's it going? What's new?" She rubs her neck with a look of revulsion. She hates remembering the past.

Oswaldo senses something different about her. He is the leader and oldest member of the group. It is thought that his body is protected by a voodoo spell since he has been involved in at least a hundred robberies without a scratch.

"You're actin' strange..."

"Me? No way? Gimme a beer. Beautiful sunset, wasn't it?"

"I didn't see it. I just woke up."

"Too bad. How 'bout you, Teleco?"

"Yeah. Fuckin' incredible."

Oswaldo gave his friend a look of annoyance. Teleco knows he abhors filthy language.

"You go by the cemetery?" Oswaldo asked Brenda.

"No."

"This is it. Just what we been waitin' for. Japa been talkin' to this dead guy's secretary. I called the gang for a meet."

"Did he say how many wakes there are?"

"Just two right now. But there's four parlors reserved. We're gonna need people."

Brenda nods in agreement.

"I've got to go keen in a little while. Elias is off."

Oswaldo is suddenly wary. He knows Brenda. She's hiding something. All he needs is for her to pull something now.

"Got everything worked out with the guard," Teleco advised.

Brenda looks at Oswaldo in disbelief.

"He's in on it?"

"No. Someone's gonna get him out of the way for me. Ok, what's goin' on? I don't like secrets."

Brenda downs her glass of beer.

"Elias wants to marry me."

Teleco guffaws, covering his toothless mouth.

"Marry?" Oswaldo repeated. "You two off your rockers?"

Brenda sees where he's headed. It's typical of him to have his suspicion meter turned on full blast.

"We've been going together for a few months. What's so crazy about that?"

"What if he finds out..."

Brenda doesn't let him finish the question.

"Today's my last day. I'm through."

"What about your nightclub act?"

"Oh, I'll keep that going. I have to work. He's just getting established. He doesn't earn much."

Teleco is afraid to ask questions. He lost a tooth in a fight with her. Brenda's got spunk. When she gets a row with someone she comes out on top.

"You gonna give up keening?" He finally gets up the nerve to ask.

Without looking anyone in the eye Brenda responds:

"No way. I made a vow. I'll always be a keener. Until my old man comes home."

She wonders if they have wakes in the United States like in Brazil. Someone at the club claimed there's no such thing in France anymore. Bodies are put in a refrigerator for three or four days, and people don't stay up all night with the deceased. She'd never go there.

"So what time are we meeting?"

"We'll work out the details before you go to the club. At ten."

She and Oswaldo had an affair. She was in love with him and she got hurt: she discovered he was married. If there's one thing she insists on, that's it. No married men. She refuses to be the other woman. He fooled her for almost a month; his wife had gone up north to Recife to visit her family. Oswaldo promised he'd leave her, he made a big fuss so she'd go back to him, but Brenda wouldn't budge. After that she didn't have the slightest interest in getting involved, until she met Elias. He'd never been married because his mother was an invalid and someone had to take care of her. He also said it was because he hadn't met the right woman. He demanded total honesty. If she was a whore, he deserved to know. Brenda asked him if he'd still love her if she was a whore. Elias thought about it for a few minutes and said: I wouldn't marry you. He accepted her working in the club; after all, it was a job. But making love for money, no way. He wanted to have children with the woman he loved. And who says whores can't have children, she asked, with a touch of irony. He wasn't amused. One of her boyfriend's serious faults is that he lacks a sense of humor.

She looks at Oswaldo with something like tenderness.

"I'm in love. This time I want it to work. It's my last day with you folks. I'm splitting."

7

The circus truck drives slowly through the city. It's lit up like a dressing room, with those lights around the cab. The artists and ring attendants stand on both sides of the coffin. An inattentive passerby might think they're advertising the show. That's exactly what one of the transvestites working General Jardim Street thinks when she waves at the circus troupe.

"Marvelous people. I just adore them."

Menendez and Paquita exchange knowing glances.

"What's wrong with you?" The magician asks the midget, who is suddenly subdued and morose.

"I'm tired. I don't see any point in this miserable life."

"You need to find a woman."

And who would want a midget, he would have said if he dared. No one understands that he would never have a mate, unless he were rich. Like a singer surrounded by tall, beautiful women. Once he fell in love with a trapeze artist who was apparently interested in him... She was forever inviting him to have dinner and go shopping together. Her name was Luna Barrios. She had one of the sweetest smiles he'd ever seen. A smile that made you want to cry. He wasn't sure if it was a smile of tenderness or pity. One night—they were in a restaurant—Tiny decided to declare his feelings. He'd even bought a suit and patent leather shoes. She praised his snazzy outfit, ordered her food, and said she had a secret to tell him. She trusted him; he was her true blue friend. The midget felt his blood run cold when he saw what she was leading up to. And so, he missed his one chance to speak.

"I'm going away. I got an offer I can't refuse from the Mexican Circus."

"Does Menendez know?"

"Of course not. I'll tell him when I'm long gone. By letter. Otherwise, he'll show me the contract and... In the Mexican Circus I'll be working with the best trapeze artist..."

"You already know the man..."

She sighed.

"Yes."

"Since when?"

"Last year. I waited for the opening. His partner got pregnant and everything was arranged. She's married to the magician."

If only he had the courage to ask if she was in love. She obviously was. Good thing he kept his mouth shut. Luna Barrios looked him straight in the eye before she asked if he was happy for her.

"No, because I'm going to lose you. Yes, because your career is important. The Mexican Circus is doing great. But I'm going to lose the one person I care about most."

"Really, sweetie? It's so nice to hear that. I want you to be a member of my wedding party."

Which was not to be. Luna Barrios sent one letter, two cards, and that's all. She disappeared without a trace. Perhaps some day... But the midget's given up hope. It's going to be a problem for him to find a mate—he envies Irene and Sandro, holding hands. The clown's twin brother can't contain himself. Could he be jealous?

"They could show some respect for the deceased."

One of the trapeze artists decides to defend the couple.

"How so? Alfredo killed himself because he wanted to. He could have stuck with me, for example. When he dumped me for Irene it really hurt me, but here I am, living and breathing. Isn't that right, Tiny?"

"Nothing worse than being a zombie."

The midget's statement puzzled Menendez. What did he mean by that? He gazes longingly at the contortionist, and she returns the look. Paquita observes her son's flirtation indifferently. Some day he has to get married. If he hasn't done it yet, well, he hasn't had the time.

The passersby in the street pause to watch the circus truck park at the cemetery. It's so cheerful. Shortly sounds of astonishment emanate from the funeral parlor as the circus troupe arrives with the coffin: Menendez and the magician are the pallbearers in front and the lion tamer and Sandro in back. The startled looks of Giuseppe Appia's friends and relatives seem to exclaim: You mean these circus people get the same kind of burial when they die?

Paquita haughtily leads the procession. She waits for the casket to be placed on the pedestal and directs everyone to sit in the chairs ringing the casket.

She inherited the crypt from her grandfather, an anti-Franco immigrant of gypsy descent who opened the first decent Spanish restaurant in São Paulo. He acquired the cemetery plot even before purchasing a house. That way he could ensure he would be buried here, rather than his body being sent back to Spain. At least as long as Franco was alive. And he wanted a plot in the city's most expensive cemetery. If some day a relative came to visit his tomb it would leave the impression of a successful life. There's no doubt that the crypt, made of black marble, and containing eight vaults, is imposing. The only piece of the family inheritance that son Paco didn't gamble away. Everything else he lost: the restaurant, the bakery, the store. He didn't even succeed in running out on his debts by fleeing the country with his family. His gypsy heritage was too strong. He loved that life. He became a street vendor selling trinkets near the train station. And he never stopped gambling. Paquita clearly remembers a period when he won enough to buy a car and a comfortable life for them. They even made plans to go visit their relatives in Spain. A sweet and fleeting illusion. He won and lost.

But it was through gambling that Paquita met Josef Menendez. His father lost a poker game to her father, and he invited her family for a good time at the circus. It was a revelation to Paquita. At that time the circus still put on plays and Menendez was the lead actor. She was almost eighteen. Either her father gave the marriage his blessing or he would lose her forever.

Paquita did nearly everything. She began as a tightrope walker and an actress. Later, pregnant with Diego, she became a clown to hide her belly. Eventually she learned animal taming and fire eating. She was called upon whenever an artist couldn't go on. With teachers like Karl, the German tamer-mime-singer, and Josef Menendez, she couldn't help but learn. And she was happy, even though her husband drank. He was affectionate and he understood and nurtured her Gypsy side, the need to keep moving. Until her cancer was diagnosed and she decided to settle in a São Paulo suburb. But she would not give up living in her trailer.

Diego Menendez invites the contortionist for a cup of coffee—in spite of Paquita's disapproving looks—at the very moment when Maria Sampaio, the dead girl's mother, decides to express her condolences to each member of the circus.

"My little daughter loved the circus. She never saw the Menendez Circus because she was too ill," she says to Paquita and continues greeting people. When she goes up to the monkey Gina, clinging to the magician's neck, Maria shakes hands with both of them. The monkey gazes deeply at her, as if she understood the woman's kindness and her sorrow.

"Bia always wanted to have a... I couldn't..."

Maria Sampaio leaves the parlor, sobbing, followed by the magician, who pauses before the coffin and admires the little girl, so innocent, dressed in white.

"She looks like a bride. Is this her first-communion dress?" He asks, before kissing the dead girl. "I also lost a daughter. My only one."

One of the family members points at the monkey, who is looking oddly at the casket.

8

Brenda enters the funeral parlor. She's wearing the same tight black slacks, white shirt, and leather jacket. If it weren't for her high heels and brown wig, people would think she's a man. She gestures to Japa down the hallway at the coffee shop, as if to say, I'm here, and she heads toward the Appia family wake. She doesn't look at anyone, not even at the body, and begins keening in a loud theatrical voice.

"Ours is such a sad lot. When we least expect it, death comes and carries off such a kind person, such a good friend, dearly loved by so many people." Brenda takes a hanky from her pocket, covers her head, and goes way over the top with her crying.

"Who's that woman, Luigi? Do you know her?" Joel goes over to his brother.

"I have no idea. She must be from the construction company."

While Brenda cries, she surreptitiously checks out the family in mourning: rings, bracelets, necklaces, and watches. This place is going to be packed with high-class types later on. It's now or never—

she reassures herself.

Marina, the daughter, instinctively sits down next to her mother, about to face her loneliness. A woman she's never seen before crying so sorrowfully over her father. This is not a good sign! She clearly remembers the day when she was arguing with her father because she wasn't eating, and he said that a woman without a rearend and breasts wasn't a woman. This business about being skinny is something the queers cooked up. Those designers make the clothes they like to wear. That's what it is. Why would they want to make their competition look better? Intelligent women don't fall into that trap. Marina, dear, eating is one of life's pleasures. And her father really did know a lot about food. He could make an osso buco that'd make your mouth water. And the sauces he came up with! No, he'd never want a skinny woman like her. But, my goodness, the miserable creature is crying so loud!

"Lord, in your divine mercy receive"—Brenda checks to see if it's a man or woman—"this loved one. Now go, brother, rest in peace."

And she leaves the parlor, her hips swaying, wondering if she's ever seen the dead man before. In the night club, perhaps? She enters the solitary corpse's wake without a pause in her convulsive sobbing.

Luigi Appia is really impressed with Brenda. When she passes by in the hallway he gets up.

"Ours is such a sad lot, when we least expect it death comes and carries off such a kind member of the family, such a good friend, dearly loved by so many people." She covers her face and sheds copious tears, while she examines, as if in close-up, the circus folks' bare necks, arms, and fingers. (The boss lady's wearing a gold watch and a wedding ring.) They stare at that strange mourner but show no surprise, is if all that were part of death's performance. Tiny is spellbound.

"May the lord, in his divine mercy, receive"—she checks the dead person's gender—this loved one. Now go, brother, rest in peace."

The artists suddenly break out in uncontrollable laughter. The midget applauds. Brenda hasn't counted on this. She shrugs indifferently and goes to another parlor. But she gives up when she sees it's a child's wake...

"The keening's rough tonight, Japa. Give me a glass of water.

Doesn't it all seem kind of strange to you?"
Japa keeps his face expressionless as he pours.
"Lotta high-class folks gonna show up after midnight. They told me to make a plenty of coffee."
"There's a dead guy all by himself. That's weird."
"You meet up with the others?"
"I'm afraid that..."
"I saw a lady with a diamond ring you could trade in for a house."
Japa's eyes close as if he were dreaming.
"Too many people."
"That makes it worth the trouble."
"I don't know. Those circus people over there..." Brenda sees Tiny approaching and she deliberately turns her back.
"Quinzão will take care of 'em."
"I've got to do my show. Bye."
The midget waits for Brenda to cross the hallway before asking who's the girl that just left.
"The best keener in the city," Japa answers. "Ain't anybody around can carry on like her."
"But why does she do it?"
"They say it's a vow. And she picks up some change. Used to be two of 'em... The other one hung herself."
"Oh, if I'd known... She cries beautifully. I'm going to talk to Menendez."
But he notices the boss over in the corner whispering to the contortionist, a Chinese girl who learned her art before her parents emigrated. She has talent. And the boss is looking for a woman. As far as anyone knows he hasn't had one for years. He's a good guy. Some complain that the pay is lousy and he exploits the artists. What boss does any different? Besides, since he settled in São Paulo the circus has been doing poorly. People are broke. They walk away from the ticket booth because the price has gone up and they're short of dough. Menendez has made arrangements with the government to turn it into a circus school.

9

Brenda looks out at the night from her apartment window. The temperature has fallen. The motionless stars seem painted on the sky. She feels something in her mouth and her belly she can't define. Hunger? She opens the refrigerator. There isn't anything to tempt her appetite. Besides, she doesn't like to do the show on a full stomach. Anyway, who's got the time? She grabs an apple and takes a bite. Elias was offended when she told him not to come over tonight. He was suspicious. She lied and said her mother was taking in the show and spending the night with her. If everything works out, she hopes she won't have a problem convincing her mother and her boyfriend that the trip to the States can't be put off. There're lots of transvestites impersonating women, but the other way around is rare. She doesn't know of a single case in São Paulo—she's the only one doing impressions of male singers. If she's lucky enough to perform in a high-class place, certainly... If Elias is really in love then he'll take off to New York with her. And if he refuses then he's not. If the holdup is profitable... Too many "ifs" in this deal. She's fed up with all the hassle, with all the petty crap—she looks at her watch. Stopped. She winds it and turns on the radio.

"There has been a fatal car accident on the Beltway. Newswoman Mara Domingues is dead. Listen in for further details in a few moments, on the ten o'clock newscast."

The traffic reporter, Brenda realizes, while she slips into a tight pair of jeans. Poor thing. Better if she'd died in a helicopter accident... Not in a car crash! That's awful.

Her face washed, she brushes her short hair, grabs her jacket, puts money in her pocket, slams the apartment door shut, takes the elevator down, walks a block—unrecognizable with those men's shoes and tough brisk gait—and enters the bar.

"I've got it. There're four wakes. Lots of people."

Oswaldo looks her straight in the eye.

"Piece of cake."

"There's one dead guy all alone. For sure his family's going to show up. We need two people for each parlor." She feigns self-assurance.

"Japa'll help."

"I can bring the bouncer from the club. He'll go for it."

Oswaldo agrees and tells her he'll take care of everything else. Brenda queries their partners. Everything cool?

"Stop boozing it up, Teleco. Last time you really screwed up."

"I'll take care of him," Oswaldo insists.

Teleco opens mouth, full of rotting teeth. He's not so ugly when he doesn't laugh. His problem is he can't hold his liquor. He gets reckless and aggressive, while he's normally shy, even cringing. The son of a mailman, eight brothers and sisters, he never learned how to read and he ran away from home. He lives a pathetic existence in a slum tenement in the Bixiga district, when he could be with his family on a small farm in Pernambuco. There it would actually be possible for him to save up to open Paradise, his grand dream, the bar where he'd sell rum and on Saturdays he'd organize dances in town with his brother who plays the accordion.

"What about Quinzão?" Brenda asks. "Why isn't he here yet?"

"He went to look for some grass and pick up his brother-in-law who's gonna pitch in. Everything's set."

Brenda eats a codfish croquette and downs a brandy before she leaves for the club.

10

Bepi Appia found out about his damned illness a month ago. He was in a meeting at the firm studying his son's plans for a building when he answered the phone and was informed that the doctor wanted to see him in his office.

"Does it have to be today?"

Yes, said the nurse on the other end of the line.

"I'll be there at six, then."

Bepi was worried but he didn't want to let on to his son.

"It like it, Luigi. How many apartment units are there?"

"Forty, in addition to the four choice suites."

"Don't sell the penthouses. This time keep them for us."

Luigi looked curiously at his father. Something was wrong with him. What was this business about suddenly keeping the penthouses? Gothic Construction had a file of special clients who normally reserved them when a building was in the planning stages. They knew it was a respectable company, not only because of its fine taste, but particularly because of the quality of the construction. Never, in the one hundred and thirty buildings they'd put up, had the firm received a single complaint about leaking ceilings or bathrooms or warped doorframes or floors. His father had entrusted to him inspection of materials and construction work.

"It's up to you to protect our investment and the family name."

His father had regretted not getting an engineering degree. He hated to study. He was capable of great sacrifice, he worked harder than anyone in the company, but studying was not his forte. His knowledge came from experience. If his father gave him an opportunity, he would repay him with total dedication. Which was what he'd been doing.

Joel was the son with a degree, but it was in dentistry. He'd wanted to be a dentist since he was a child. An unusual calling. Quiet and sullen, Joel was hard to get along with. He didn't like going out; he passed up even vacations and weekends away from home. He hated Christmas parties, birthday dinners, in fact, celebrations of any kind. Perhaps because he refused to wear a suit and tie. Even to his own graduation ceremony, to the consternation of Bepi Appia, who couldn't understand his son's attitude. Why was he so aloof from the family? Why didn't he get married? Why this, why that? Over time, Joel was left alone with his secret life. He showed up when he felt like it. And no one in the family felt comfortable going to him for treatment. Marina took the college entrance exams three times but finally gave up. She'd never pass. Then she joined a friend in his veterinary clinic and now she's in charge of the canine section. If she has to she can give shots, dress wounds, and assist in operations and in putting away sick, blind, or old animals. She earns more than her husband, a cinematographer who never knows when he'll sign his next contract. Francesca, although she was very attached to her father, made him very sad when she went off to study acupuncture in Japan. The last time they spoke on the phone she mentioned she had gone to visit Kyoto with a friend. Her father, fearing the answer, avoiding asking who he was. Why acupuncture? She could have studied medicine. It would have made him so happy. Francesca was determined. Her father had to understand that it was her future they were talking about. It's what she wanted, period.

"Sir, those ladies from the museum are here for the meeting."

Bepi hurriedly stood up.

"I completely forgot. Please, interrupt me if we go past five thirty. I've got a doctor's appointment at six."

"Any problem, father?"

"Just a routine check-up. I've been having dizzy spells and some times I see double. I consulted a neurologist. We'll talk about those penthouses later on."

His son greeted the three women and the photographer entering the office. Three elegant ladies, married to successful industrialists, who devoted their time to promoting art and opera in São Paulo.

"We've come to deliver the medal you were supposed to receive at the ceremony," the oldest said.

"Health problems. Actually, that was the day I had to go to the doctor."

"You must not get sick. Who is going to take care of our opera?"

Giuseppe Appia smiled proudly.

"You would soon find another sponsor."

"No, sir, don't say such a thing. No one loves the arts as you do. And no one could ever replace you in our arts organization."

Her companions agreed. The photographer made ready to document the medal presentation ceremony. Bepi Appia looked out the window as if he were seeing another continent.

"Men pass, art remains. My family comes from Sapri, a small village in southern Italy. My great grandfather was a postal worker, and my grandfather was a fishmonger before he came to Brazil. A simple man who loved music. He wanted me to be a singer. He wanted a famous grandson. My father used to sit me in his lap and tell me I was going to give class to the name Appia from the province of Potenza. But I didn't have any talent so I couldn't make his wish come true."

The oldest of the ladies gave him a sympathetic look.

"Be that as it may, you certainly have made the Appia presence known in Brazil. Your name is inscribed in our city's museums, libraries, and theatres. That is why we have come to express the appreciation of the Friends of Arts Association." She hands him a velvet box containing the medal.

"Thank you very much. But I haven't done anything." He stood up and opened both doors of a shallow cabinet where hundreds of medals and decorations were pinned.

"I hope to see the project for the construction of our new theatre approved in a week."

The photographer used the occasion to take what would be the last pictures of the distinguished patron of the arts.

At the doctor's office, Giuseppe Appia finally discovered the cause of what was bothering him: four brain tumors.

"I'm sorry, my dear fellow. You insisted on knowing."

"I can't stand physical pain."

"I know, Bepi. I'll do what I can. I promise." The doctor got up to put away the x-ray.

"You can't imagine how painful the truth is to me. Lucid for another month. Just a month."

"The sooner you make arrangements..."

Giuseppe Appia thanked him as a friend and as a professional for his honesty. He would appreciate it if no one in the family found out about it for the time being.

"I'll tell them at proper time."

Two weeks later he was celebrating his thirty-fifth wedding anniversary with an intimate supper. Joel made a rare exception and showed up. His father had a surprise for all of them.

Bepi, acting very serious before the dinner, gave each of his children an envelope, putting aside Francesca's. He handed his wife a small box.

"Vera, the engagement ring I was unable to give you. You've been a wonderful wife."

"Don't tell me you're going to make a public spectacle." Vera laughed and opened the box. "It's lovely. But it's huge. It was so silly of you to..."

"Promise you'll never take it off."

"I'll be mugged at the first corner I come to. How can I wear this on the streets of São Paulo?"

She kissed her husband affectionately and sat back down.

Each of the children received one of the reserved penthouses. Their father asked them to stick together always, even after his death. And he had to rush out of the room so they wouldn't see him cry.

On the eleventh of September, Giuseppe Appia told his secretary he would be unavailable and he locked himself in his office. He wanted to be alone to write his goodbye letter.

Dear Vera, dear children, I am sorry for what I am about to do, but I have no other choice. In a few days I will no longer be lucid: malign tumors are growing inside my head. I prefer not to suffer. I love all of you. Thank you. I was (and I am) a happy man. Think about me from time to time. All my papers are in order, my will has been prepared. Goodbye.

The next day he walked into a hotel, requested a room, drank several scotches, and shot himself in the chest.

11

At the wake, the widow looks indifferently at the ring. She's not crazy about jewels. She'd rather her husband had shared his problems with her. But that's the story of their life. As if women couldn't think. In fact, he once told her that she didn't have to think, all she needed was to look pretty and feminine. She was obviously offended. Who wouldn't be? She always deplored her husband's Italian Don Juan side. Whenever they went to a dinner he flirted with the woman sitting next to him or with the lady of the house. An obligation.

"Sweetheart, it makes women happy. Compliments let them go to sleep feeling confident. Who does it hurt? It's an act of generosity."

And he would give a self-satisfied laugh. She finally accepted him for what he was. He also tried his flattery on her. Pointlessly. She had more than enough to keep busy. The Saint Francis of Assisi Orphanage relied on her, on the money she acquired through parties she gave and the government support she gained. Two hundred and fifty children. Why should she care if her husband went through with his seductions or not?

"There's a monkey hiding inside every man."

That's exactly what she thought. Her husband could interpret the sentence any way he wished. That girl who cried in front of his casket, was she one of his lovers? Hard to imagine. So skinny. A man's body. And she fancied her ring—she looks at the diamond again. She'll do something useful with it. With so much mugging and robbery, plus the economic crisis, it's not fair to wear a fortune on her finger. Forgive me, Bepi, but tomorrow I'm selling the ring and donating the money to the orphanage.

Vera Appia's thoughts are interrupted by the arrival of friends in evening dress.

"We heard about it after the opera. The director of the theatre asked for a moment of silence for the great patron... He gave a moving speech."

About thirty people have come directly from the performance. Some will be back again tomorrow for the burial, others have professional obligations. She understands perfectly. It's quite alright.

Japa checks his watch. Midnight. The perfect time for the gang to get here. Never in his life has he seen so many necklaces, bracelets, and rings all in one place. And there's still an hour to go! Brenda's show should be just starting.

12

Brenda, sitting in the narrow dressing room at the end of the hall, has just put on her make-up. She still has to pin up her hair, put on the man's wig, paste on the moustache, and apply the bright-red lipstick, which will transform her into an ambiguous figure, neither man nor woman, in spite of the white suit and bow-tie. She's heard the buzzer and she's hurrying to go on stage. The first song will be sung in the dark. Is this one of those nights when she feels inspired and sensual? She hears her hoarse voice fill the room. In a short time, under a single spot-light, she's going to do the best strip-tease in her life. She'll slowly take off her tie, jacket, belt, pants, shirt, bra, and panties. She doesn't even care if there's a full house; after all, the economic crisis has gone from bad to worse and who's got a dime to spend? She just wants to sing—to impersonate her beloved stars, as if the impersonation made her as much a star as Caetano Veloso... Oh, if she could sleep with him just once. And she has another dream: to see Ney Matogrosso in the audience during her act, the one who inspired her—the other way around—to create her character. *Death in Venice* was also influential, with that man dying his hair, being made up... What's that author's name? The most incredible movie she's ever seen. Some day she's going to buy a VCR and see *Death in Venice* a zillion times. Or do those jerks think she's too dumb to appreciate a film like that, hm? When she's doing her show, like now, she imagines she's being filmed, and that's why she has to put all she's got into every gesture as the camera does a close-up, her eyes shut, singing "Body and Soul," while she unbuttons her pants and lets them fall to floor... They ought to make a movie of her life story. She should write it down for someone to make a script out of it. If she goes to the United States... Success can be hers there.

The applause echoes loudly. The people who've seen the show like it. But the audience is so small tonight. She better get going: she grabs her robe and runs to the dressing room.

There really isn't any future in this place—she thinks as she wipes off the lipstick and puts on a denim outfit and tennis shoes. She's splitting and never coming back. Enough is enough. Some people have the Midas touch, they're so damn lucky. Just the other day she ran into an old school chum who married a cousin whose father's a baker in France. They opened a bakery and it was such a hit they had to expand the business. Amazing. Now they've got several stores all over the city. Money. That's what she needs: money. Then she'll show them what she can do. Ok, she's in love with Elias, but nothing in the world is going to stop her from going to the United States. Nothing.

That's that. From this moment on she's another person. She's got a new role to play. And this time it's for real. She's been involved in two robberies, rehearsals for tonight. They were cheap-ass burials, good learning experiences. They ripped off so little that on one bothered to complain. With what she netted from the first one she bought her record player, with the second she took two weeks' vacation in Guarapari. But she cut it short because she didn't want to make her father sad in prison. She usually visits him on Sundays. Poor old guy. For some reason hard luck follows him, and he was denied parole. By next month he will have done his time. How's he ever going to adjust to life in the city? She's planning to leave something for him before she takes off. Tonight's stickup is crucial. The way it works is you put everything in a sack, sell the jewels, and divvy up the dough. But if she can get her hands on that widow's diamond ring... It's worth a fortune! With that ring she'll... She feels ice in the pit of her stomach. She won't let herself think about it.

Brenda ties her tennis shoes, buttons her jacket, checks to see if the moustache is glued on, puts on her cap, shuts the dressing room door tight, leaves quickly so no one sees her, and jumps into the cab the bouncer's hailed for her.

13

The full moon floats through the mist beginning to form and casts its pale light on the cemetery. Looks like the dawn is coming, Nando thinks as the closes the door. The cold night wind won't do Dito any good. He picks up the bottle of rum and gives his companion a swallow to soothe another coughing spell.

"How you doing?"

"Weak. Tired. Did I sleep?"

"A little."

"I must have passed out, Nando. I don't remember a thing."

"You moaned a lot. Where's it hurting?"

"My chest and my back."

"First thing in the morning I'm taking you to Mercy Hospital," Nando promises, as he takes down the clothes hanging on the line, folds them, and puts them in a bag.

"Did I vomit blood again?"

Nando notices his friend shivering with cold and his eyes are bright with fever. He nods his head, certain Dito won't see his response.

"What time is it?"

"Quiet, Dito. You don't want to start coughing. Must be a little after midnight."

"If I make it to tomorrow."

"Don't be ridiculous. Want me to heat up some coffee?" Nando recognizes that the situation is going from bad to worse. Dito's in bad shape. And there's nothing he can do about it. Can't even take his friend to the hospital, since the cemetery gate stays locked all night—the watchman goes home to sleep. If they ever catch... Poor fellow. Watch what? If he did his job, Nando and Dito wouldn't have a place to live. Or is he just pretending he doesn't know? Nando is certain that a few days ago the watchman saw him carrying in a cardboard box and a blanket. After all, it was a large box. How could he fail to notice? Maybe his pretending he didn't notice anything was a simple matter of generosity. Several times Nando bought rum for him because his tooth is always aching. He also got some pain pills for him from one of the girls at the drug store. A nice southern girl. Yesterday he asked for some cough syrup and cold medicine for Dito when the owner was out for lunch. To rob a robber is not robbery. She smiled when she handed him the medicine. Nando didn't get what she said. He wasn't paying attention because she's so pretty, so... He could spend hours, days, weeks, years on end looking at her. She's so blond and her eyes are so blue. She looks like a princess. A fairy. No, a saint. She's exactly like that Madonna in the Consolação Cathedral, the one with those red circles on her cheeks and the painted eyes. Exactly. He suddenly smells the coffee and quickly takes the mug off the burner.

Dito holds it in his trembling hand and gestures for his friend to put something underneath his head. Nando picks up the clothes he's been folding to use for a makeshift pillow and then lights two candles.

"I've got a son, Nando."

"You? Really?"

"With Elisabete."

Nando tries to remember her face. He once saw Dito sitting on a park bench with a fat dark-haired woman. He hid behind a tree. He didn't want his friend to think he didn't know how to mind his own business. It made him laugh because the girl was so much taller than Dito.

"Where is she these days?"

"She went back to Córrego Manso. Her father's a stonecutter and he lives close to my mother's house."

Dito has talked about his home town, about the watermelons they planted to feed the pigs. He laughed about the fact that people in São Paulo bought thick slices of the fruit to eat.

"He go with her?"

"Who?"

"Your son, of course."

Dito takes a sip before answering.

"Sure."

Nando has his doubts: he just made up that story about the son. He's delirious. Why didn't he ever mention him before? Why would he hide that from a close friend?

"What's his name, Dito?"

"Who?"

"Your son."

Dito's eyelids droop in exhaustion. They stay closed for a few minutes.

"Expedito da Silva. Like me."

So it is true. He really does have a son. But how, when, where? Nando wishes his friend would tell him. It would be so nice if they could have a conversation. If Dito were well...

"Did you get married?"

"No. That's the point..." Dito's movement brings back his coughing. "Will you do me a favor, Nando?"

"Anything."

"If I die, will you register him for me? I don't want him to be a kid who doesn't know who his father is. Will you go to Córrego Manso and say I recognize him as my son and..."

"I promise. Don't worry. Did you ever see your son?"

He nods and his cough is so prolonged Nando becomes nervous.

"Elisabete had him in her aunt's house in the slums. She went home so she could take care of the boy."

"Hush."

"I want my son to know he had a father."

"You leave it to me. But you're not going to die."

For the first time Nando doesn't believe his own words. It seems unlikely his friend will make it through the night. Without god's help.

14

The gang waits at the corner by the cemetery. Teleco can barely stand. He shouldn't have drunk so much, but how could he face the stickup without drinking? Oswaldo's worried. He knows Teleco. He's not meant for this. He's part of the ring because he doesn't have a choice. He has to finance his trip back home.

"You see those rich dames went in? Jewels bigger'n my fist. If Brenda don't show up..."

"She's on her way. Keep your cool," Oswaldo urges.

"Last time we waited she didn't show, and..."

"She'll make it tonight."

Quinzão passes the marihuana around. He's the only one with a police record. Arrested one day, released the next: lack of evidence. He's always dressed in jeans and a leather jacket, whether it's cold or hot. Maybe he sleeps in his clothes. No one's ever seen him in anything else. He's got who knows how many kids, unacknowledged, in the city's slums. But he's got a job as a driver for a daycare center and he likes children.

"I saw a brunette go in. She's mine," he says. "I'd even marry that one."

"Cut the bull, Quinzão. Ain't no chick's gonna buy your line." Teleco laughs.

"Knock it off, for Chrissake! This's gonna be quick. We'll be in and out in three minutes. Before you can blink. Got it? Three minutes. Here comes Brenda."

Teleco opens the paper bag and passes around stockings and weapons.

"Pull the stockings over your heads. What you waitin' for?"

"Hi. This is Cobra." She introduces him.

Muscle-bound, Oswaldo thinks, before explaining that he'll cover for them in the hallway next to the door.

"You spell everything out, Brenda?"

"Yup." She covers her head. With the shadow of a moustache, who would guess that...

"Then let's go."

They cross themselves.

The man who ran into the hearse in the afternoon offers his condolences to Bepi Appia's widow. He's come from the Municipal Theatre and he's apologizing because he won't be able to attend the burial, an important meeting in Rio...

"It's quite alright, my friend." Vera offers her cold hand. "Thank you for coming at such a late hour."

His wife leans over the coffin to kiss the dead man. No one there knows that she and Bepi were lovers in their youth. And they would have gotten married if her father hadn't been so vehemently opposed—why? She couldn't understand. She went on a hunger strike; her father was a cruel monster. She was a minor, she had to obey. For a while they exchanged love letters, with his sister, a high school student, acting as go-between. She was madly in love. But suddenly she saw a picture in the paper of Bepi and Vera Appia's wedding. False-hearted... Her father was right. As she leans over one of her diamond earrings drops into the casket. Oh, my god! How's she going to find it in all these flowers?

While she furtively searches for her jewel, hidden in some rose petal, a band of mask-wearing thieves bursts into the wake.

15

"Everybody up against the wall. We're not gonna hurt nobody," Oswaldo shouts. "Put your jewels and money in the sack." Cries of alarm everywhere. Luigi rushes to his mother's side. Quinzão interrupts the next wake where the circus folk, half asleep in their chairs, fail to grasp what's happening immediately. The magician covers the monkey's eyes and Paquita clings to the midget. How could such a thing happen during a wake? Brenda keeps Menendez, Joel, the dentist, and a friend of the Sampaio family covered at the coffee shop. Teleco keeps an eye on them while another gang member passes around the sack. Japa, pretending he's not involved, puts the money from the cash register into the container Brenda points to and then puts his hands up.

"Can't you even respect a place like this?" Someone shouts.

"Hand over that pin, lady, we ain't here to play games."

In the front parlor people continue to give up their jewels and cash. Everyone knows someone who's been held up. It happens every minute in São Paulo—the woman who lost one of her earrings hands over her ring and necklace. Oswaldo points to her ear with the pistol barrel. She takes off the other earring, attempts an ironic smile: this was inevitable. Her husband shows them his empty wallet: besides his watch, nothing. Luigi empties his pockets, filled with money. He has of course come prepared to pay expenses, the grave diggers' tips and the coffee shop bill. Very Appia tosses the precious ring in the sack.

"You can't have my wedding rings. You'll have to kill me first."

"Shut your trap, lady. Take that thing off." Oswaldo is irritated.

The circus people are paralyzed with fear. Paquita gives up her gold chain and watch and yanks off her wedding ring with loathing. Quinzão suspects she's hiding something between her breasts and he points at her brassiere with his pistol. She hands over the bills hidden in a greasy handkerchief.

"If the government can steal from us and freeze our bank accounts, then why can't these people who don't have a thing steal, too?" A female relative of the dead child shouts.

"Anybody moves gonna blown 'em away."

The contortionist, on her way back from the rest room, flattens against the wall. There's a gun pointed at Menendez. Quinzão approaches her and forces her to walk over to the cabinet in the back of the coffee shop. Menendez is about to resist when he feels the barrel from Brenda's pistol press against his neck.

Quinzão fondles the terrified contortionist's breasts.

"Leave the chick alone, Quinzão."

"I'm gonna make it with you, cutie."

When Menendez hears these words he can't contain himself and lunges. How dare anyone say such a thing to his lover. Brenda is startled and shoots without thinking. Menendez topples to the floor.

This wasn't supposed to happen. It wasn't—Brenda thinks in a panic and turns to Japa for support.

"I said there'd be a screwup," Oswaldo shouts. "Quick, shut the doors. This's gonna cause big trouble."

"We'll be seein' you around," Teleco says defiantly before running off.

After the robbers make their getaway the contortionist throws herself on Menendez.

Someone suggests calling the police: the public telephone cord has been cut. Who? When? Was Japa the last one who used it? Who can say?

Paquita screams when she bends over Diego Menendez: he's dying. A clean shot to the heart. It's all over. She takes out a plump breast and lays her dead son's head on it. If someone asked her to explain she'd be unable to. It's a reflex action. As if she had just given birth.

Tiny kneels, lift's up the dead man's pants, removes the concealed wad of bills, and gives it to Paquita.

"If you want I'll take care of things."

It takes the police two hours to arrive, even though the station house is only a few blocks from the cemetery. What else is new? After all, the police have so many armed robberies to deal with. Actually, there is something new: the location. But the detective realizes that once the newspapers get hold of the story the idea is bound to catch on.

"This is an unfortunate crime. The question is how to react in a situation like this? This fellow went to the movies, didn't he? There're plenty of TV shows showing how this kind of bravery gets you in trouble."

"My son hated television, officer. And he didn't care for the movies. It was in the cards. It was his destiny to die this way." Paquita sighs.

Diego Menendez's body is carted off for the autopsy.

"If it weren't for the crime scene this'd be just another senseless robbery," the detective repeats to Luigi Appia. "There's nothing we can do about it, my friend. We're undermanned, the pay's ridiculous, and I wouldn't be surprised if any day now the police started committing robbery, too, just to survive."

Luigi Appia is not amused by the inappropriate witticism. He ends the conversation by turning his back on the policeman. Then he hears his mother's hysterical fit of laughter, a harsh, piercing laugh. It frightens everyone, as if something worse were about to happen— her sons embrace her, perhaps out of shame, or fear, losing two loved ones, one to death and the other to madness, would be too cruel— Luigi looks at his mother in terror, Joel takes a pill out of his pocket, quickly brings a glass of water, and forces his mother to take the tranquilizer, since he is now in charge and she must follow orders. At the same time, the Italian relatives are speaking in loud voices and complaining: "porca miséria, questo paese non é sério, qui no se po piu vivere, madona mia"—This is hell, this is not a serious country, this is no place to live, for god's sake. Everyone is? up in a arms about economic policy, things are bound to get worse, the president of the republic is off his rocker, someone's got to stop him from any more nonsense, industry's in bad shape, workers are starving, hope for better times is fading, the country's got so much potential but it's poorly run, how can anyone feel like working and producing? Those are the words of an Appia family friend who's asked for the floor. Some of the circus folk have gone to the next parlor to listen to the speech, while the unlucky wife sticks her fingers into the wilted flowers in the casket, maybe she can at least find her earring. What a bad idea to wear real jewelry to the theatre, she could have used her fakes like her friends, those were only ones left (for a long time now she's been selling things, with the factory in trouble). Which is why she's tried to keep up appearances, anyone who knows diamonds can tell the difference, only fools are duped by paste diamonds.

Paquita remains motionless as she listens to the demented laughter and the inflammatory speech. She thinks about what will become of her, who will come to her aid, perhaps the dwarf, so devoted and obliging. If he wants... No, she doesn't dare to even think. She's been hurt the most. While they've all lost something, she's lost Diego, brutally murdered: how can she live with her sorrow?

She doesn't have the courage to die with him; she's alone in the world. Tiny shakes his head, takes the boss's hand in his, and gives her an affectionate kiss—she has to take care of the circus artists, they are her family, now more than ever, she doesn't have anyone outside the circus, and they can give each other strength and face Diego's absence together. Paquita must calm down and trust in him and the others, her faithful friends.

In the parlor where the dead girl lies, the relatives are huddled together and speaking in low voices. But Maria Sampaio also decides to inveigh against the Americans and Germans who've come to exploit the country and give nothing back, buying off crooked politicians, taking our every last cent, the last drop of blood of a submissive people who ask for nothing in return. Then a former colleague takes offense and he sides with the bosses, she's talking nonsense, that talk is old hat, what we need is to get some police protection in this city, we need to get rid of corrupt politicians, people pay taxes but their money isn't invested in social welfare and security.

Sérgio Sampaio sobs uncontrollably, till now he's put up with his suffering in silence, his sister thinks, a sorrowful, gasping cry, a man crying is always the saddest, she doesn't know why. There, bent over his daughter, what is he mourning, the loss of his little girl, the emptiness he'll feel inside forever, or is it remorse over having refused her the videotape, the feeling that he's money-grubbing and selfish? He and his wife won't be able to stand the video rental shop anymore, they'll move to a new home, street, city.

Japa serves sugar water and listens to the comments, his indifferent expression unchanging, betrayed only by a taut muscle making his mouth twitch and closing his left eye. Brenda was crazy to shoot. How could she... Incredible. Self-controlled, efficient Brenda. Something bad must have gone through her mind. Something very bad. When he leaves here the first thing he'll do is ask her where the loot is. She could do something stupid, rip off a gem... Who knows what they actually got? The group has a solemn agreement to sell everything first and afterwards divvy up the take in equal shares. If anyone dared to trick the others... He better not think about that. What's he going to do with his share? Oh, a lot of things. He'll move to Mato Grosso. He'll buy himself a spread. Farmland's cheap there. His mother's complaint suddenly pops into his head: his habit of never completing his sentences. Yes, he'll take along his father, mother, and brothers and sisters. There'd be more hands for field work and tending livestock...

The detective interrupts his thoughts.

"Any coffee? Holding up funeral parlors! If this catches on..."

16

Dawn has come to São Paulo. Images pass through Japa's mind: maids hosing down patios, chauffeurs polishing their employers's cars, children on the way to school, workers waiting for the bus. The city is still enveloped in mist at Japa's favorite hour: daybreak. Friends and relatives of the deceased who have left to take a bath or freshen up are slowly returning, their hair damp and their appearance restored. The circus folk have stayed at the wake, their faces stamped with the double sorrow and the strain of the vigil. Diego Menendez's coffin has just arrived. Several policemen now patrol the cemetery. What for?—Japa sighs. Some habits in this country he'll never understand.

The detective stands before the solitary corpse and remarks to a journalist who has just interviewed him:

"I wouldn't like to have nobody to cry for me after I'm gone."

The journalist smiles and agrees.

"That guy was a bad apple. A jerk. He spent his whole life fighting with everybody and his mother. He sucked up to the government and fed from the public trough. Once he got what he wanted he'd try to dump his sponsor. They say he couldn't get it up or he shot his wad too soon, something like that. What I know is he was a son-of-a-bitch. At the newspaper we knock on wood when his name's mentioned because he brings bad luck. He married for money. His wife was ugly as sin. She helped him play his dirty tricks. They had a son, a fag. A soon as he realized it he sent him abroad. He worked for politicians who supported torture; he wrote speeches for them in the expectation of rewards that never materialized. He was resentful and envious and misfortune followed him around. The robbery last night must have happened because he's here. I swear. He had a persecution complex. He wouldn't turn his back to anybody on a restaurant, no matter who it was. He'd pick the table in the farthest corner and make sure he sat against the wall, but even that didn't stop his nervous habit of looking backward. Once a colleague wrote something negative about him in an article and he went to demand an explanation. During the argument, in the middle of the editorial room, he foamed at the mouth like a dog with rabies. No, I don't think anybody'll show up for his burial."

"Sounds like you knew him pretty good. Was he a friend of yours."

"He pretended to be, the jerk... If you'll excuse me, officer, I'm going to pay my respects to the deceased."

The journalist goes up to the casket, spits in the dead man's face, and leaves the parlor—the white spittle remains in plain sight.

The detective asks people to leave their names and addresses with his assistant for the necessary affidavits.

A patrolman arrives with the news that four suspects have been arrested trying to steal a Mercedes. The police van is on the way to the station.

"Were the jewels on them?"

"No. Just money."

Japa overhears the conversation and trembles as he serves the coffee.

"Watch out," the magician advises. "You don't want to burn yourself."

The policeman studies the crumbling white face make-up and

the worn black frock coat.

"To think there're countries where graves are desecrated!"

"Is this the first time the funeral parlors've been robbed?" The magician asks.

Japa lowers his voice to answer.

"I don't think so. The guy whose shift comes after mine had an experience... but nobody got killed..."

"Where were you during the stickup?" The detective demands.

"Here. With a gun pointed at me..."

The magician backs him up him and moves aside for Luigi who asks for a glass of water.

"How long have you been working in the coffee shop?"

"Two months. I was living in Rio. Things got tough. Wasn't no work, here at least I can eat and pay my rent..." His mouth twitches nervously again.

"That girl who was here in the afternoon, she come every day?" Luigi's voice is a bit unsteady.

"Who?"

"The keener." Tiny helps out.

"Often."

"She get paid for her crying?"

"Sometimes. But there's some people don't understand. If some-one thinks she might've been the dead person's lover, well then... They call Elias, the guard. He takes her outside and comes back to collect the tip."

"She aware of this?"

"Maybe. They're friends. Everybody at the cemetery likes her. Even the grave diggers..."

When Japa's replacement shows up he takes off the cap and dust coat.

"Man, ain't it unbelievable?"

"I'm not sure if I'll be in tonight. I'm beat."

On his way out the police officer calls him over to fill out a report, which Japa dreads. He can barely write or answer the questions. He's in a hurry. He wants to get over to Brenda's and let her know that there've been some arrests and it might be the boys. Stealing a car was part of the plan.

"Sign here," the policeman orders. "Your full name."

"Japa Kawata."

"Is your name really Japa? Sounds like a nickname."

"But it's not."

He crosses the street. He's sweating. Being so close to the police would make anyone nervous. He walks faster but then to avoid calling attention to himself he waits at a bus stop—no, he's not being followed. He tries to take a deep breath and slows his pace until he reaches the corner. Whew. Now he'll go in through the garage—the attendants are never there—and cross the inner courtyard. Japa looks up and checks out the apartment. Brenda must be there.

17

The dense fog totally obscures the window. He takes the service stairway and pushes the elevator button.

Japa imagines Oswaldo, Teleco, and Quinzão—who could the fourth person be?—running through the city until they get to the parking lot. Oswaldo's specialty is car theft, with a piece of wire he takes just a minute, if that, he's seen him hotwire hundreds of cars, he loves teaching other people how, but you need a light touch and Quinzão doesn't have it, his hand is too pudgy, his fingers are short, it's no use, Oswaldo, this ain't for me, you gotta learn, dammit, any kid can do it, that's the point, if I was a kid maybe... Try, Quinzão! His partner's crazy to insist, it's the wrong time, he's enjoying himself, danger gives him a rush. Quinzão sweats as he pushes in the thin wire, he tries once, twice, it just won't work, Oswaldo laughs and with a flick of the wrist, only one, he opens the Mercedes. They could have picked a less conspicuous car, dumb to waste nervous energy on petty crap, don't take no longer is Oswaldo's excuse.

When the elevator doesn't come, Japa decides to walk up all

twelve flights. Where's he going to find the strength? His legs are rubber, he hasn't eaten anything since yesterday except for a ham and cheese sandwich, he hasn't felt hungry lately, he's gotten thin, he used to be husky... he can't show up in Rio looking like that, he doesn't want to worry his mother... he's got to sell a gem fast—they don't pay much in the Praça da Sé—besides, the heist'll be in the newspapers, the fences'll close up shop, maybe he could catch a bus and go sell it in a southern state like Paraná, if he's not well dressed any jeweler will know the piece is stolen, no, he's got to buy some clothes, he needs to pose as a rich dude, but it looks like the money's history... if there were four arrested... Deep down he doesn't believe it, it must be a coincidence, Oswaldo wouldn't let them arrest him just like that, he'll go to the meet at the Praça da República, he's sure they'll all be there, and he'll show up with Brenda, how many flights left, ten?... he's short of breath, it's tough working nights, he presses the elevator button again, where is the goddamn thing? he gasps in the effort to catch his breath, his throat's dry, a sharp pain in his left side, like the one he felt when he lost Sakae, the love of his life, how could she have ended up in Japan, far away and out of reach? One afternoon he thought he saw her in the street, arm in arm with a girlfriend, he could swear it was her, the same walk, the same pinned up hair, the yellow silk dress he'd given her, there was no mistaking her walk, he ran up from behind and threw his arms around her tightly, the startled transvestite didn't appreciate it and punched him in the face, he broke his nose in the fall, the fracture still hurts when it rains... eight flights... And Sakae had married a cousin and taken off for Japan, pointless to stay in Brazil, there she'd earn more in a month than she could in a year working her fingers to the bone in a small factory here, no lunch break, inhuman exploitation, they promised overtime but didn't pay, that's no way to live, and she couldn't stand seeing street people anymore, kids operating as purse snatchers and pickpockets, she was robbed sitting on a bus, she didn't even notice when they cut through the leather strap, when she got up her purse felt strangely light, they had taken her whole purse, appalling, imagine if she knew what her former boyfriend is up to now, her leaving was for the best, he'd lose his nerve, he has to get out of this shitty mess once and for all, but he misses her so much, they loved each

other, she'd never care for the other guy like she did for him, never...
Six flights. What if he stopped for a while, his legs hurt, someone
opens a door, he flattens against the wall, are you nuts? you want
people to think you're a thief? but isn't that what you are? he keeps
climbing, the maid on the seventh floor smiles at him, cute, hm?
sudden hard-on, he ignores it, since Sakae went away he hasn't
touched another woman, and the girl might scream, wake up the building, he's there for another reason, to look after the take from the
holdup, before somebody does something stupid... But what if
Brenda's not home? They'll all get a fresh start, no one's born a crook,
just the opposite, but who can put up with misery forever? All his
partners have their own story... But Brenda, she's a mystery, so pretty
and intelligent... he gives her credit, people are so complicated, that's
why he prefers animals, he'll fill the house with dogs, cats, turtles,
monkeys, birds. And a horse. That's a must. He's nuts about animals.
Only a few stairs left, but the pain in his left side has increased, he
feels faint, god help me, he breathes deeply, he's so hungry, hope
Brenda's got something to eat, so dizzy, weird, come on, one last
push and you're there, Japa Kawata, ok, the pain's going away, ring
the buzzer.

He waits a few seconds and tries again. Is Brenda asleep? The
buzzer'll wake up the neighbors. Godammit, open up quick.

He hears noise in the apartment. He knocks on the door. What
if Elias is with her? How's he going to deal with that? He'll pretend
that...

"Just a minute. I can't find the key. Who is it?"

"Japa." He's almost whispering.

She appears at last. She's wearing a night-gown, her hair is
down and it's so... Another hard-on.

"You do you want?"

"You alone?"

"Yes."

"The gang's been arrested."

"I don't believe it."

Japa sits in the armchair. Brenda opens the window and a dense
fog drifts into the room—she wishes it were a cloud—she picks up a
brush and leans against the bed. He sees at a glance the bag of loot on

the table.

"That's impossible. Who told you?"

"A cop showed up at the wake saying four suspects were arrested trying to steal a Mercedes. I'm not sure..."

"That's all we needed." Her brush strokes are vigorous. "This time everything's gone wrong. Maybe it's a coincidence. Oswaldo wouldn't let himself get caught so easy."

"That's what I think, but... That's what I heard..."

Japa picks up the paper bag.

"Where you gonna hide this?"

"Why hide it?"

"Anybody'll talk under torture."

"For god's sake, Japa. You'll bring us bad luck." She knocks on wood three times. "Everybody'll keep their mouth shut. Maybe I can ask Elias..."

"Get the police involved? You crazy? Cops mean trouble," he says, picking up the package.

"Elias and I are getting married."

Jappa appears to ignore her announcement.

"Any prime stuff in here? Married! If he finds out you killed that circus owner you can kiss your marriage goodbye. Where's the other earring for this set?" He dumps the contents of the bag on the table.

Brenda nervously tosses aside the brush.

"It should be there. Teleco handed me the package on the way out. I haven't messed with it. You think that earring's genuine?"

Japa examines the stone.

"Guaranteed."

"Those rich bitches usually wear imitations. They keep the real stuff in a safe or in the bank. I bet this's a fake." She picks up the earring, puts it on, and looks at herself in the mirror. "But it's very pretty. I want to wear it for my next show."

"You know how the deal works. Sell everything and split the money."

"No one's going to miss an earring. If you don't say anything... Pick out something for yourself, too."

"A deal's a deal."

"There's a gold Rolex in there."

"Gold?" Japa's expression changes and Brenda thinks he's taken the bait. "How would you know? You said you haven't... What's going on?"

She turns around, the watch isn't there, she rummages through the jewels looking for it, shit, she finds it on the floor.

"This one."

Japa tries it on.

"Classy. Horseshit luck the cops getting the money. How we gonna sell...? I need money. I promised I'd send some to my mother."

"Sell the watch."

"What with a murder, the cops, and the press, we're gonna have to wait a long time or we'll give ourselves away. Where's the diamond ring?"

"What ring?"

"The widow's."

"I don't know anything about a ring."

"The rich widow. That ring I said you could buy a house with."

Brenda paces back and forth. Japa is aware of his partner's anxiety and pretends to look through the pieces on the table.

"How much bread you think they had?" She tries to gain time. She hadn't counted on his remembering the ring.

"I don't know. Wasn't much, enough to get by, enough to..."

"With all this stuff we'd be set for life." Brenda takes a gamble. "Especially if we divide it between two of us."

"Two?" Japa asks seriously.

"You have any idea what this earring's worth if it's really high quality? And the watches? There're six expensive ones, plus the gold chains and bracelets..."

"God forbid... The others." He intentionally stops in the middle.

"Fuck them. Who's to know? We'll hide out for a few days and then we'll catch a plane and split for Buenos Aires."

"So where we gonna sell this stuff?"

"In Buenos Aires. We'll make a killing. I'll take off for the United

States and you can buy that land in Mato Grosso you've been fancy-ing."

"Where's the ring. You took it."

Brenda hesitates a few seconds before lying.

"I didn't take it. Everything's there."

Japa looks outside; the fog is beginning to thin. He's absolutely certain she's lying through her teeth.

In his mind betraying the gang is wicked. Betrayal is the worst crime a human being could commit.

"I saw the widow turn over the ring and then spit on Teleco."

"You saw that?"

"Yes."

"Then Teleco put the ring in his pocket."

She hopes she's planted doubt in Japa's thick head.

"Teleco? I'd swear by him."

Anyone else might hide a gem like that from his partners, but not Teleco. He's not smart enough.

"Oh? Well, I don't swear by anyone. Not even my mother." Brenda goes over to the window. She feels hot.

"I swear by Teleco." Japa approaches her aggressively. "Got shit for brains. Faithful as a dog. Either you..."

"What if the ring did disappear? Who took it?"

"I don't trust you... You tried to throw me off with that earring and the watch..." He pulls a stiletto from his stocking.

"I wasn't expecting you here so early. And I wasn't expecting anybody to get arrested."

"Where's the ring?"

"I don't know," Brenda responds.

Japa grips her arm tightly.

"If I find out you're double-crossing me like you double-crossed the others, you won't get out of here alive. I use this blade to kill stinking double-crossers."

Brenda presses seductively against him.

"Don't be a drag, Japa. Let's get out of here before the police show up. They must be looking for us by now. If anybody snitched on me, then they said you were in on the stickup, too... Think about it... We'll sell something, buy the plane tickets, and..."

"Without the ring, no deal." He opens the closet and begins rummaging around the shelves.

Brenda tries to relax with a few dance exercises. She put away her clothes so neatly, the blouses and t-shirts folded and stacked as if they were in a store, it's stupid of him to mess everything up—she feels like crying. God forbid he should find anything. Forgive me, Elias, but I've got to get away. If it's true the other gang members have been arrested, it's time for her to split... Quinzão's a blustering coward. Do it, put out for Japa—she intentionally lifts up her night-gown and shows her legs and breasts to turn him on. He's removing the hangers, inspecting each item of clothing, fingering pockets, cuffs. Brenda turns pale.

Suddenly, the overcoat... The stiletto rips open the lining: the jewels spill on to the floor.

"So you were gonna keep the cream of the crop for yourself?"

"I must have lost my head... I'm sorry... You can keep it all. It's not in the cards for me yet. Give me a watch so I can take off..."

Japa seems to be thinking, his eyes shut tight to conceal his thoughts.

"You know the rules."

"Don't hurt me," she stammers, petrified. "Look, you can make it with me if you want."

Japa pushes the button in the handle and the blade flips open.

"I don't like you and your man's body don't turn me on."

Brenda looks around, terrified. No way out. What if she threw herself out the window? She's had that thought many times. She'd experience the sensation of flying for a few seconds. Since childhood she's dreamed of opening her arms and flying. But Japa's holding her so tight from behind she'll never get loose. She tries to move and the blade plunges deep into her belly. Once, twice, how many times? Brenda sees herself tiny, in her mother's lap, riding bicycle with her father, the day she stood enraptured before a Christmas tree all lit up, coming during the rape, and finally dressed in a white tuxedo, singing, the audience applauding. Suddenly, she no longer hears her own babbling voice.

"There's nothing beyond... Nothing."

Japa has the strange sensation that he can feel Brenda's soul escaping her body, a kind of thick, white blotch drifting by the window, as if it didn't want to leave.

He puts away the knife and the jewels and glances quickly at his partner. What do you know, he forgot the earring. Japa keels down, and feeling no revulsion, yanks it off her ear, which is still warm. And he hears a moan. Whose?

18

At the cemetery, a few graves have been opened and the grave diggers await their dead. No, no one's resting in peace here, at least not on this Friday, when the fog is fouling up traffic and the drivers are blowing their horns as if they were yelling—how can you live in the city when you have to face these hassles every single day?

The bus from Our Lady of Grace School parks on the sidewalk next to the police car, in front of the funeral chapel: the girls in uniform won't get off until it's time for the burial; they're not allowed to see the dead girl's open casket.

"Sit still until I get back," says the teacher.

Unnecessary. They know it's a cemetery, a place of silence. The driver is surprised by the behavior of the normally boisterous students.

Elias, the guard, crosses the street, he's late—he looks up at Brenda's apartment. Could she be awake? Then he remembers Brenda saying her mother was going to see her act and spend the night with her. She's bound to wake up early, which explains the open window.

What've those two guys who watch the cars done with themselves? Just when you need them the most they disappear.

No, Nando can't leave his friend alone, he's having difficulty breathing, his eyes sunken in his pale face. Even if he could pick up some change helping with the traffic and watching cars, he's got to keep Dito company—he decides as he puts away the aluminum utensils. He won't last long. If only he could stay on his feet and make it to the hospital! The burial services will start soon, the watchman must be busy, giving directions... He'll ask for his help at noon. The two of them can wrap Dito in a blanket and carry him out through the back to the sidewalk and call Mercy Hospital emergency. That way nobody'll find out they're living here—Nando looks at the protecting walls and already misses the faces in those photographs.

"Wish I had a family like that one there." He tries to make conversation and points to the framed portraits on the wall.

Eight pictures of the deceased. Except for a woman with wrinkles, they all have the same face, the same nose: the old fellow, the men, and the bride in a white gown—Nando recognizes the similarity.

"Can you see that girl? I had a girlfriend even prettier than her," he says proudly. "Maybe you don't believe me, but I did. We met in a park. She was tiny and olive-skinned. I could cover her face with my hand. She was the only person who ever really kissed me. The only one who loved me and I loved her."

Nando stops talking but Dito gestures for him to continue.

"Her mother wouldn't let us stay together and she moved away with her daughter. Don't know where. With good reason. She deserved somebody better'n me. Sometimes when I'm thinking about her I feel like crying. Her name was Nena."

Dito smiles with his eyes.

"The old guy has a nice grandfatherly face, don't you think? A kind grandfather. The old lady I don't like. Got a mean face."

Dito makes an effort to see the photographs again, but he shakes his head dejectedly.

"What's wrong? Feeling worse?"

"No. I'm almost past the point of feeling anything."

"It's funny. Every time I think of Nena I see a field full of fat cows. A real green field, with the cows grazing way off. I don't know why." He puts away the aluminum plates as if he were tossing his thoughts in the bag. He gets up to open the door He needs some air. His friend! His breathing is deep and slow. Nando has a lump in his throat.

19

Giuseppe Appia is the first to leave the funeral parlor for the Bueno e Silva family crypt. And the coffin isn't to be opened again, at the widow's request. But when the grave-diggers are about to lower it, they're interrupted by the butler's unexpected display.

"Oh, boss, please don't leave me. I care about you so much. The kindest man I ever met. What'll become of me! I want to kiss that dear hand one more time. Please, madame."

Appalled, the widow gives her consent.

A few onlookers can barely contain an explosion of laughter brought about by the butler's effeminate blubbering.

The casket is opened and Giuseppe Appia is duly kissed by his bereaved employee. Vera Appia sadly listens to someone laughing.

The singing of the school girls in Bia Sampaio's cortege drowns out the guffaw, which sounds as strange as if it had come from Bepi himself. Vera realizes she wouldn't put it past him. He was always the same impertinent Italian.

Should auld acquaintance be forgot,

And never brought to mind,
Let's drink a cup o' kindness yet
For auld lang syne.

The voices drown out the sound of the traffic as the families wait for the workmen to close the graves.

Nando smokes to repress the urge to cry and hopes for a miracle that will make Dito get well. He's so weak he has to speak softly and conserve what little strength he has left—he signals for his friend to come closer.

"I think I'm going to heaven. I can hear the angels singing."

Dito laughs and his head falls back.

All over. Nando paces back and forth, then pauses before the photograph of the old man: won't he whisper a piece of advice? He can also hear the angels singing. Is it possible? He pushes the door wide open. He sees the girls in their uniforms and someone directing the choir. He has a broad view of the cemetery from the crypt and takes in all the burials, my goodness, so many people. It's a good thing Dito thought he was at heaven's gate. At least he was happy at the hour of his death. Nando feels his eyes brimming with tears. Dito didn't ask to be born, his luck was all bad, and he died too young and poor. At least he heard the angels sing.

He then makes a decision: he will keep the promise to register Expedito da Silva as Dito's son. Maybe he'll be luckier than his father. Nando comes back inside, covers the body, picks up his things, and slams the door.

20

The circus troupe leaves the cemetery and climbs into the truck. Paquita, holding hands with Tiny Vieira, looks forlorn. She tries to take one last backward glance before passing through the gate.

"Please, Paquita, don't look back. They say their souls'll stay with us and won't find any rest. You've got to take care of us. And the circus."

Paquita refuses to believe her son is dead. She has the impression that when she gets back to the trailer she'll find Diego. After all, dying in a funeral parlor is so absurd that if she hadn't seen it with her own eyes the hold-up would be nothing but a nightmare. Dreams are so real sometimes... She refers to her son as if he were alive, waiting at home.

And what if she turns around abruptly and finds him there?

"This is what I'm going to have inscribed on his tombstone: 'He has gone to entertain the dead in the celestial circus.' What do you think, Tiny?"

He doesn't answer. Those are the words of a poet. He looks admiringly at her. A poet.

The Sampaio family is saying goodbye to their friends.
"Thank you, girls. I'm sure Beatriz appreciated your being here."
The mother senses that the image of her daughter decomposing will haunt her nights for a long while. She'll think about the rotting flesh, the worms, the bones that will someday be delivered to her in a plastic bag. The clacking of those bones will sound repugnant to her ears, like the time they delivered her father's bones. She felt nausea rather than nostalgia. Who was that man in there? she asked. But she knew the answer. It's so hard to face the truth.

Her husband believes in resurrection. And in reincarnation. In life after death. Not her. The only meaning her daughter's death has for her is monumental failure. From now on she will envy every mother with a healthy child. She remembers an acquaintance whose son was a junkie saying she'd rather see him dead than in that hopeless condition. Imagine that. At least he was alive. Anything is possible.

Beatriz is dead and gone. Never again. Death is lodged in the mother's heart. The wounds inflicted on her soul will never heal. No, she won't have anything inscribed on her daughter's tombstone. She'll never come to visit her, she declares fervently to her husband. He's got to understand.

The couple walks along the main pathway of Memorial Cemetery. He promises himself he'll come visit Bia every day. He's overcome by a strange sensation: she's not really dead, because he's alive. Hard to explain, but that's what he feels. When the period of mourning is over he'll talk to his wife about another pregnancy. It'd be a way to bridge the chasm of silence that has opened up between them. A nearly insurmountable silence.

Which doesn't make sense. He'll try to take Maria to the theatre. Just like old times when they wanted to be actors. They even started rehearsing "Our Town" at the club. But the director, who was a professional, had a falling out with the management. Who ever heard of putting on a play about death? That was a place of recreation. Comedies and nothing else. Beatriz was conceived during their honeymoon. Their passion for the theatre would have to wait its turn. Maybe in a few months, who knows... He'll discuss it with his wife.

Yes, he'll come to visit his daughter every day. And he'll have her epitaph inscribed. All human beings have a right to an epitaph. Where did that idea come from? So do animals. Beatriz was six when Brigitte, her setter, ran across the street and was run over and killed. They buried her in the yard. Brigitte received a gravestone, which the azaleas covered.

He's going to think up an epitaph that says something about his daughter's gentleness.

21

The Appia widow asks her children to go on ahead. She wants to be alone for a few minutes—she sits on the edge of the grave. The sensation of death suddenly hits her. Or more precisely, suicide. Bepi put an end to his life without the slightest compassion toward her. Self-reliant to the end. Vera would like to have been his friend. He kept it to himself: fear of looking ridiculous? He even had to be funny making love, the wop Don Juan, the loving father with a heart of gold, and selfish S.O.B.

No, they were never in love with each other, but they had fun together. She's going to miss him; his raucous laughter will never again echo through the house. And miss Sunday lunches, his delicious risotto, the family standing around the stove with him stirring the rice and everyone praising his broth. Yes, she'll miss that cheerful, vivacious Italian. A lot. His courage surprised her. She never imagined he was the sort to kill himself. Because, by god, it takes courage to pick up the gun and pull the trigger. Black humor. She can't explain it, but she feels like laughing. The butler's farewell

141

scene...

She's going home to do what needs be done. Perhaps she should take over the firm. But she has no intention of abandoning the orphanage. And she needs to put everything that's happened out of her mind. The robbery, the stupid death of the circus owner, the image of that woman trying to breast-feed her dead son. An image that touched her deeply. Why?

Someday, maybe not far off, she'll join her mother and her husband. She believes devoutly they'll meet in eternity. Otherwise life would be futile and sad. At least for her. She remembers their trip to Italy, the excursion to Sapri to meet the family, the climb up the mountain. The wind blew and the trees swayed gently. The ruins of what had been a stone house. There was so much serenity in that corner of the world that in spite of her youth she thought she'd like to be buried in such a peaceful place, to turn to dust in that natural setting.

Unfortunately, her wish won't be fulfilled—she stands up and takes the main pathway. Just as it was impossible to fulfill her mother's wish to be buried in a library so she could amuse herself while she waited for Judgment Day. The funeral parlors are empty and clean. What could have happened to the solitary corpse?

Her oldest son has been waiting for her at the gate.

"I just found out that keener is dead. Murdered. She was the girlfriend of one of the cemetery guards."

"Oh! That girl? Heavens."

"At dawn."

"Another one?"

Vera Appia, who until this moment has kept control of herself, puts her head on Luigi's chest and cries. Who is she sorry for? Herself? The girl? All the people? The nation?

There's nothing special about this dawn. It's a morning like any other. We have to admit the truth. He caresses his mother, following with his eyes the helicopter flying over the cemetery.